INDIAN AND CHRISTIAN

Historical Accounts of Christianity and
Theological Reflections in India

INDIAN AND CHRISTIAN

Historical Accounts of Christianity and Theological Reflections in India

Lalsangkima Pachuau

2019

Indian and Christian: Historical Accounts of Christianity and Theological Reflections in India – published by the Rev. Dr. Ashish Amos of the Indian Society for Promoting Christian Knowledge (ISPCK), Post Box 1585, Kashmere Gate, Delhi-110006.

© Author, 2019

ISBN: 978-93-88945-25-7

Laser typeset by

ISPCK, Post Box 1585, 1654, Madarsa Road, Kashmere Gate, Delhi-110006 • *Tel:* 23866323

e-mail: ashish@ispck.org.in • ella@ispck.org.in
website: www.ispck.org.in

Dedicated to my mother Mrs. Biakveli

and

the Churches she loves in my motherland of India

Contents

PART 2
India's Theologies in their Religious Contexts

PART 3
Christianity and Nationhood in Northeast India

Introduction

Learning to work with the contradictory strains of languages lived, and languages learned, has the potential of a remarkable critical and creative impulse. At times, the English language had the archaic feel of a carved almirah that engulfed you in the faded smell of moth-balls and beautiful brittle linens; at other times it had the mix-and-match quality of a moveable feast, like Bombay street food, spicy, cheap, available in all kinds of quantities and combinations, subtle delicacies with street-wise savour. I went to Oxford to embellish the antique charms of the armoire; I ended up realizing how much I desired street food [of Bombay]. Why was I intellectually fascinated and unmoved, when I found myself at the academic acme of the literary culture that I had chosen to follow?

– Homi K. Bhabha.[1]

It was in the busy city of Kolkata (then Calcutta) that I had that moment. It was an epiphanic moment of some kind, which I believe is quite common among researchers. I am referring to a triggered moment or just a momentary experience when something suddenly makes good sense, or when ideas just fall together logically and meaningfully. It was in the early 1990s around the time I was preparing for my Ph.D. study that I came across a term in such an epiphanic moment that explained a lot of things I was looking for at the time. I was visiting my favourite bookstore, the Oxford University Press Bookstore in Park Street. As I came into the bookstore on that wonderful afternoon, I browsed the shelves and one book on the top shelf immediately caught my eyes. Before I was helped to get the copy from the shelf, I could read only a part of the title that says "Ethnonationalism."[2] Even before I saw what was inside the book, I said to myself, "That's it!" The book itself did not impress me immediately and I found some chapters to be a bit problematic at that time. But the thoughts and ideas the term conjured in me were deeply satisfying. This term "ethnonationalism" explained, I thought, how my people and other minority "nations" like the Nagas understood their identity as a community. I took the term with me and began researching it. I discovered the works of Walker Connor on the concept[3] and followed it. A sense of reservation I used to feel with names like the Mizo National Front and the Naga National Council, which will be dealt in the last chapter of this book, were somewhat explained and justified by this term.

I often wonder if it was the experience of my generation that made the question of identity so important for me. I grew up in Mizoram at the time when several ethnic groups in Northeast India were embroiled about their national identity causing political conflicts and revolutions. Identity became the heart of the matter in my early academic inquiries. When I first planned to write my Ph.D. dissertation on "Tribal Identity," which I later changed to "Ethnic Identity," in connection with Christianity in the 1990s,[4] the question of identity was not yet as popular as today in academia. Even as I broadened my academic horizons and approaches, the theme of identity continues to occupy an important place in me.

This book is neither an exhaustive historical account of Christianity nor comprehensive theological reflections. Above all, the chapters represent thoughts on aspects of history and my personal theological sojourn as an Indian Christian. At the heart of these accounts and reflections is what it means to be an Indian

Christian. Thus, the intent is to survey the national and religious identity of Indian Christians historically and theologically. India as a nation has been trying to define its identity in a variety of ways. The contributions of a new intellectual group often clubbed together as Neo-Hindus have been significant. As much as I sought to understand the identity of my Mizo people, I have also been trying to understand India's identity as a nation to which my identity is established or to be established. Alongside this quest for ethnonational and political identity is the question of Christian identity in India. Chapters in this volume are written from the perspective of one who seeks meaningful connections between these three identities, namely being Indian nationally, being Mizo ethnically, and being Christian religiously. The first part deals with questions generated by the interaction between Indian nationalism and Indian Christian self-understanding and works. Indian Christian interactions with nationalism went beyond their role in the freedom movement. I understand Indian Christian thought including its theology to be greatly influenced by Indian nationalism, even though the national majority is often less than favourable to Christians.

Before tracing how Christians conceive their nationality in the changing times (chapter 2), I first want to examine how Indian nationalism relates to Christians (chapter 1). To cut to the chase of nationalist view on Christianity in India, I jump to Mahatma Gandhi as the nation's leader-hero to extract the heart of nationalism's attitude on the rise of Christianity. Gandhi more than represents India; he is the heart of Indian nationality. His moral authority and national leadership have been a great partner in the formation of my ideas. He is not only a national "Mahatma," but also a thinker with whom one can have meaningful conversation. Inter-religious conversion has become the controversial issue surrounding Christianity in India today. This is largely because Gandhi made it the core issue in his criticism of Christianity especially for the Dalits (or "Harijans"). Thus, we focus on conversion to understand Indian nationalists' encounter with Christianity.

In the second half of chapter 2, I trace the development of Indian theological thought as influenced by the rising national consciousness in independent India. This development has been either punctuated or halted at the present time by rising Dalit-tribal theology on the one hand and the surging Hindutva that threatens secular India on the other hand. We end the account of theological development with the nationalist story. The dynamism and complexity of the present theological development as spearheaded by Dalit and tribal Christianity is beyond the scope of this work. Yet, I need to acknowledge that all the chapters in this book are written from that perspective.

To many practicing Indian missionaries today, missions as a foreigner's enterprise has long passed. Perhaps intimidated by rising nationalist thought within Indian Christian communities, the story of how the Indian government blocks the entry of foreign missionaries to India has not been much considered. While in theory there is a route for foreign missionaries into India via "missionary visa," it is now practically impossible to enter India as a missionary. As shown in chapter 3, information on the government's eventual closure of missionary entry to India has been sparse and vague. If the ceasing of foreign missionary operations in India beginning in the late 1950s was thought to be the end of Christian missionary works in India, it definitely was not. We will deal with the story of Indian missionary movement in India in the ensuing period. The peripheral nature of the missionary enterprise in India seems to have hidden this vital movement. For quite some time, it is true to say that there are more missionaries in India than ever before, and most—if not all—these missionaries are Indians. Though occurring as it does on the margins of historical churches largely among independent evangelicals, charismatic and Pentecostal Christians, this movement is beginning to transform Indian Christianity.

India has a long, rich and unique theological history. The uniqueness of Indian theology lies in the active participation of Hindus who engage Christian thoughts as Hindus. Furthermore, the diversity of Christian practices and thoughts shows the richness of Indian theology. From the ancient Syrian orthodox church with its pre-Chalcedon theology to the newest form of Pentecostalism, the spectrum spreads from one end of Christian type to the other. The two chapters in part two are intended to exemplify the variety and types by showing two theological examples with some depths. The two chapters show two very different kinds of Indian theology from a historical viewpoint. The first one (chapter 4) deals with Neo-Hindu readings of the Bible and shows the face of a Hindu Brahminic theology on the gospel. The second (chapter 5) is on the development of a distinctly tribal theology shaped by the primal worldviews and ethos of the Mizos. Both are theologies that emerged out of the gospel's interaction with non-Christian or pre-Christian religions, yet very different kinds and in different contexts. The two chapters also represent two contrasting viewpoints. While the chapter on theology and primal worldviews is a theology in a context where Christians are a large majority—all the Mizo people are now Christians, the context of the Hindu reading of the Bible is where Christians are in a small minority. One chapter shows a theology from a non-Christian viewpoint and the other shows how a theology came to be formed for a people group who consider themselves highly Christian. If the descriptions of aspects of Hinduism and Mizo primal religions in some details are bewildering, I ask you to be patient. The points are built from the religious descriptions and they are clearer in connections with the religious features narrated.

Part three of the book deals with Christianity in relation to national identity in Northeast India. In chapter 6, I relate the origins of Christianity in different parts of Northeast India. I have two related purposes in this chapter. The first purpose is on a historical method, that is, to show how a conscious historiography that is sensitive to both the indigenous mind and the missionary contributions may function. The second purpose is to narrate the history of Christianity by giving due place to the forgotten major players in the story, namely the native Christian workers right from the beginning. There are a number of writings on the history of Christianity in Northeast India, and I try not to repeat them. I purposefully call it "re-scripting" as I try to retell the story from an insider's viewpoint. Christianity has been accused of having played clandestine roles in the political turmoil of Northeast India. As will be mentioned, even liberal-progressive leaders like Jawaharlal Nehru blamed foreigners, including the missionaries. In opposition, I firmly believe that it is the sense of the people's identity, their ethnonational feeling, that is at the root of the problem. Both as an insider and as a Christian, I venture to interpret the issue in the last chapter.

Each chapter of this book can be read independently, while together the chapters form a whole viewpoint. All the chapters have their own stories, and I owe a depth of gratitude to all who have played important parts in their compositions. Chronologically, the last three chapters (7, 5, and 6 in that order) were written first. Soon after I joined the faculty of the United Theological College in Bangalore, back in 1998, students from Northeast India at the college organized a meeting where I presented an earlier version of chapter 7. The paper was published later in *Bangalore Theological Forum*.[5] I presented the earliest version of chapter 5, "Theology in the Mould of Primal Worldviews," at the faculty research seminar of the United Theological College in November 2003, and I thank the faculty members and students at that time for enriching interactions. A revised version of the paper was published in *Missiology* in 2006[6], from which I rewrote this chapter. Chapter 6 as titled here "Re-Scripting a Christian History" represents my historiography and the story I have retold several times.[7] An earlier version of the paper under a different title was presented at a Seminar on Christianity in History [of India] of the Centre for Historical Studies, Jawaharlal Nehru University, New Delhi in February 2011 which was later published in 2016.[8] An earlier version of chapter 4 ("Hindu Reading of the Scripture") was published in 2013.[9]

All the chapters in part 1 (chapters 1, 2, and 3) are part of the larger sabbatical project I had in 2010, which was my first sabbatical leave from Asbury Theological Seminary. The chapter on Gandhi (Chapter 1), however, has a longer history. Beginning in the reading of *Gandhi's Truth* by Eric Erikson in one of my doctoral seminars for the Ph.D. at Princeton Seminary in the early 1990s, I began pondering about Gandhi academically. I investigated Gandhi's way of integrating Indian values and Western thoughts as a theoretical model during the writing of my Ph.D. dissertation. During my sabbatical leave from the United Theological College in 2004, I spent a year at the Center of Theological Inquiry (Princeton, NJ) as a research scholar and I did a study on Gandhi and Christianity among other things. I presented the earliest version of what is presently chapter 1 at a seminar in the Center. Daunted by the spirit of "Mahatma," I hesitated to publicize my critique on Gandhi presented here for a long time. During my next sabbatical leave in 2010, I revisited the piece on Gandhi as a part of a larger study I was launching. I presented an earlier version of this chapter as the Montagu Barker Lecture, Oxford Centre for Mission Studies on February 16, 2010, which was later published in *Transformation*, the Centre's journal.[10]

I spent four months of my sabbatical leave from February to May of 2010 as the Scholar-in-Residence at the Crowther Centre for Mission Education of the Church Mission Society in Oxford, UK through which I was also a visiting scholar at Regents Park College of Oxford University. Much of the research and initial writings for the first part of this book (chapters 1 to 4) were done during that time. I especially thank my friend Dr. Cathy Ross for making possible that rich experience. In addition to my service at the Crowther Centre, I was privileged to present my thoughts in several institutions, one of which was at the Oxford Centre for Mission Studies mentioned above. An earlier version of a section of chapter 2 was presented as the Drysdale Memorial Mission Lecture at Nazarene Theological College, Manchester, on March 24, 2010. Another section of what became the same chapter here was also presented at York St. John University in its research seminar series for the faculty of Education and Theology on May 20, 2010. My presentations at the Wisdom in Mission Conference of the Henry Martyn Centre of Cambridge University, at Leeds Trinity University College, at the Faculty Seminar of Redcliffe College, Gloucester, and interactions with students and faculty of Trinity College, Bristol where I was an academic visitor for a few days, helped germinate the thoughts presented in these chapters. I remain ever grateful to Dr. Peter Ray of Nazarene Theological College in Manchester, Dr. Kang San Tan at Redcliffe, Dr. John Corrie at Trinity, Dr. Kirsteen Kim at Leeds Trinity, and Dr. Sebastian Kim at York St. John for their kind invitations and hospitalities.

After I completed much of the writing of Part 1 during my sabbatical leave in 2010, I was privileged to present the works to an Indian Christian audience in January 2011. At the invitation of Principal Rev. Richard Rodgers of Leonard Theological College, I delivered earlier versions of chapters 1, 2, and 3 as the annual Bishop and Mrs. Parmar Lectures on Ministry and Mission in India at Leonard Theological College in Jabalpur, MP, India. The faculty and students responded with stimulating questions and encouraging comments and the whole event was a great and rich experience for me. I thank my friend Dr. Atola Longkumer for initiating the process that led to this event, and I am ever grateful to Mrs. Sunita and Rev. Rodgers for hosting me warmly in their home with all the special meals of gourmet cuisine quality! Leonard College's authorities hoped to publish the chapters as a book but had to give it up due to financial difficulty, and I acknowledge their initiative that led to the present volume. May I also record my gratitude to all editors and publishers of the journals and books where some of these chapters had appeared for their permissions to publish them again in this form.

As I complete the writing of this book, I have just renewed my Indian passport claiming my Indian citizenship. Keeping Indian citizenship while living and working in the United States has become quite costly in different ways for me. Yet, there is an inexplicable "impulse," the kind Homi Bhabha mentioned in the above quotation that made me work earnestly to keep my Indian identity intact even in the face of occasional unfriendly treatment from the Indian authorities. After years of working in Western institutions and churches, something like what Bhabha calls the "subtle delicacies" of lived realities recorded in the pages of this book kept me going as Indian and Christian.

Endnotes

[1] Homi K. Bhabha, *The Location of Culture: With a New Preface*, Routledge Classics (2004), x-xi.

[2] Arun Ghosh and Radharaman Chakrabarti, eds. *Ethnonationalism: Indian Experience*, Netaji Institute for Asian Studies, Publication Series II (Calcutta: Chatterjee Publishers, 1991).

[3] Walker Connor, *Ethnonationalism: The Quest for Understanding* (Princeton: Princeton University Press, 1994).

[4] The dissertation was turned into a book, and was published as *Ethnic Identity and Christianity: A Socio-Historical and Missiological Study of Christianity in Northeast India with Special Reference to Mizoram*. Studies in the Intercultural History of Christianity. Vol. 129. Frankfurt am Main: Peter Lang, 2002. In 2012, an Indian edition came out with the same title from Centre for Contemporary Christianity, Bangalore.

[5] "'Tribal' Identity and Ethnic Conflicts in Northeast India: A 'Tribal' Christian Response." *Bangalore Theological Forum* XXXI, No. 1 (July 1999): 157-167.

[6] "Mizo '*Sakhua*' in Transition: Change and Continuity from Primal Religion to Christianity," *Missiology: An International Review* 34, No. 1 (January, 2006): 41-57.

[7] One of the earliest versions was published as "Church-Mission Dynamics in Northeast India" *International Bulletin of Missionary Research* 27, No. 4 (October, 2003): 154-161.

[8] "'Assistants' or 'Leaders'? The Contributions of Early Christian Converts in North-East India," in *Christianity in Indian History: Issues of Culture, Power and Knowledge*, Edited by Pius Malekandathil, Joy L. K. Pachuau, and Tanika Sarkar, p. 102-118. Delhi: Ratna Sagar, 2016.

[9] "The Bible in Christian Mission among the Hindus: The Communicability and Reception of the Bible in the Hindu Context," in *Bible in Mission*, eds. Pauline Hoggarth, Fergus Macdonald, Bil Mitchell, and Knud Jørgensen. Regnum Edinburgh Centenary Series, Vol. 18. Pp. 68-80. Oxford: Regnum Books International, 2013.

[10] "A Clash of 'Mass Movements'? Christian Missions and the Gandhian Nationalist Movement in India." *Transformation: An International Journal of Holistic Mission Studies* 31, 3 (2014): 157–174.

PART 1

Indian Christianity and Indian National Identity

CHAPTER 1

Mahatma Gandhi and the Dalit Movement to Christianity in India

Clashing of "Mass Movements" [1]

Quite a few historical studies on Christians' attitudes to Indian nationalism and their roles in the nationalist movement are now available.[1] Employing what may be called a nationalist historiography popular from the 1960s to the 1980s, some of these studies are quite critical to the Christian communities, especially to their insignificant role. One influential historian of Indian Christianity, Kaj Baago, for instance, "deplore[d]" the National Christian Council for "its lack of courage"[2] to support the nationalist movement. Through the adoption of this historiography by the Church History Association of India, Christian scholarship tends to be somewhat guilt-ridden. The Indian nationalist movement itself was largely unquestioned and presumed to be virtuous as led by the nation's most revered Mahatma. The blame has been laid almost wholly on the Christians for their indifference and non-involvement. With few exceptions,[3] difficulties faced by Christians in the political condition and social setting have been considered. The dominant question has been the Christian attitude and roles on the nationalist movement. In the present project, we begin the investigation by first asking the attitude of the Indian nationalist movement on Christianity and on the Indian Christian community. By focusing on Gandhi's encounter with Christianity and Christian conversion, we trace the development of nationalist attitude on Christianity. In the next chapter, we come back to ask the Christian community's response to the nationalist movement.

Because the Indian nationalist movement was a mass-based movement for freedom from colonial subjugation, especially after Mahatma Gandhi took the reins in 1919, it has often been referred to as a "mass movement."[4] Ironically, the most dramatic increase of Christians in number before India's independence also came about under the name of "mass movement" roughly around the same time. These two "mass movements" have been treated in isolation from each other and in separate fields, and to my knowledge, have not been related with one another.

"Mass Movements" to Christianity

To describe the conversion movement to Christianity in India among the Dalit[5] (or "Depressed Class," who were formerly the "untouchables" or "outcaste" of Hindu society) and tribal communities *in groups*, or as some said *"en masse"* or in many cases *en bloc*,[6] analysts and critics have used the phrase "mass movements." Although such movements had occurred in earlier period, what came to be associated with the name "mass movements" were those which had taken place in various parts of India in the period beginning in the 1870s and ending in the 1930s. Statistics show that the Indian Christian population quadrupled during this period. Based on the Census report, it was determined that the Christian population grew from 1,246,288 in 1872 to 6,020,887 in 1932.[7] In some rough estimates, more than half of Catholic Christians and more than 70 percent of Protestant Christians in India traced their origin to one of these movements. In the late 1920s, the National Christian Council of India commissioned a study on the movements and the Chairman of the Commission, J. Waskom Picket,[8] wrote a book based on the massive study. The book remains the best empirically-researched work and one of most thorough discussions on these movements.[9] Based on the ten regional expressions of movements selected and studied by the commission, Pickett defined the movements as those characterized by "a group decision favourable to Christianity," and proposed calling each "a group movement."[10] Later studies, especially on mass movements in other regions, have revealed that this is too narrow a definition since all communities categorized under mass movements do not necessarily make such a "group decision" for their conversion to Christianity.[11] Pickett's work had a remarkable impact on subsequent theories of mission. The best known mission theory which directly came out of Pickett's work was Donald McGavran's Church Growth theory.[12] While McGavran focused on what can be emulated from such movements to grow churches, recent historical studies on mass movements in India have focused on Pickett's other point, namely how the movements helped to liberate oppressed Dalits and tribal people from the age-old bondage to the Hindu caste system.

Both within and without Christian circles, "mass movements" as a concept and a practice came to acquire strong negative reactions. Prejudices against the phenomena, which influenced much of the theology, theological education, and the church in India until the late 1980s, not only shelved away the issue for a period and thus thwarted serious deliberations on the issue, but also prevented educated Christians of mass movement origin from affirming their identity. Many educated Christians concealed their Dalit identity until recently. Describing the mood in the early 1930s, Pickett said, "the term mass movement," meant different things to different people. For some, "it has stood for hasty baptism and loose administration. To others it has been synonymous with the reception into the Church of 'outcastes' or 'untouchables.'" Still others "conceived of it as representing the conversion of the whole populace to a strictly nominal confession of Christianity."[13] Behind all these distrustful opinions is the question of its spiritual legitimacy. One can also suspect a strong influence of the caste mentality in the negative reactions.

Not only did many non-Christian Indians treat the movements and the converts with derision, "large and influential sections of the missionary body [in India] and of the Indian Church have questioned their spiritual validity and have doubted whether they should be encouraged,"[14] wrote Pickett. One may easily spot statements that discouraged and disowned mass movements by Indian Christian writings even in the subsequent period. Christian missions, which typically started among caste communities, were eventually drawn by such movements to work among Dalits. As John Webster stated, "it was primarily the foreign missionaries rather than the Indian Christians who responded most eagerly to the Dalit initiative," while Indian Christians of caste origins were "unenthusiastic and even antagonistic towards the mass movements."[15] Referring to the general Indian Christian community, Pickett also found that "large numbers of educated Indian Christians are severely critical of mass movements and assume aloof or even hostile attitudes towards them."[16] Thanks to the new initiative on historical studies of these movements since the 1970s and the new effort since the 1980s to formulate liberation theologies based on the experience and identity of the oppressed Dalit and tribal communities, the new trend is to pride instead of derision of the movements. Like liberation movements elsewhere, such as those among the Blacks (African-Americans) and women (feminist movement) in the West, many Dalit Christians now choose to identify themselves as Dalits with a sense of pride, and work for the liberation of their identity and its dignity.

What led critics and opponents in the past to oppose Dalit mass conversions was the dominant worldview that dichotomized matter from spirit, and thus temporal from spiritual life. Recent studies have shown that such dichotomy is foreign to the traditional worldview of many Dalits and most tribal people in India. Certainly, the primary clash was that of worldviews. In Sathianathan Clarke's observation of Dalit mass conversion movements, "religious conversion was also a conscious mobilization of disadvantaged communities. Religious conversion to Christianity was a community effort by the Dalits to denounce the symbolic worldview of conventional religion within which the legitimization of the all-encompassing caste-based social order works."[17] There is no denying that "the underlying motivation was the search for improved social status, for a greater sense of personal dignity and self-respect, for freedom from bondage to oppressive land owners."[18] Such a motivation in the context of the transformation to "God's people" from "no people" is legitimately religious. In an effort to counter the sceptics who suspect the spirituality of Dalit mass conversions, one Dalit theological thinker and a spokesperson for Dalit communities, James Massey, called the movements "Spirit Movements" to emphasize their spirituality.[19]

Another important observation to be made is the role of early native converts in initiating and maintaining the movements. Although Pickett did not emphasize this aspect, his brief historical description on the movements clearly highlighted the significant role played by early leaders of mass conversions. The story of Vedamanickam of Sambavar community in the Kaniyakumari district of Tamil Nadu, Ditt (converted as a result of the witness of another native convert Natu) of Chuhra community in Punjab, Yerraguntla Periah (also converted as a result of the witness of a native Christian Vongole Abraham) of Madiga community and Vankayya of Mala community in today's Andra Pradesh, are examples we can readily see in Pickett's book.[20] John Webster looked for patterns in the mass movements among Dalits and identified individual native leadership as a common feature. He identified what he calls "leader stage" in which the leadership of those among early converts helped "to lead the rest of their people to convert also."[21] As I have shown in my research on tribal movements to Christianity in Northeast India, most stories of tribal conversion there are the result of the works of early "native" converts.[22] In many cases, foreign missions had very little or nothing to do with the conversion of these leaders, and in other cases unlikely convert-employees of mission agencies also served as the instruments. In the high time of the missionary movement in India, the focus of missions had mainly been on the high caste people. After the "leader stage" of the movement, Webster said, came the mission or missionary stage when "the Mission realized that a movement was afoot and decided to deploy its own resources both to spread and to shape it."[23] Cyril Firth's earlier observation concurs with this point when he wrote, "it has been the converts who sought out the missionaries rather than the missionaries who sought out the converts."[24] The initiative taken by "native" (Dalit or tribal) converts is an important key in understanding the nature of the movements. From such a viewpoint John Webster concluded his analysis of Dalit mass movements by saying, "the mass movements were Dalit movements initiated by Dalits and sustained by Dalit heroism in the face of persecution."[25] Viewed as depressed communities' quest for salvation, the role of native converts in the movements has an added significance.

Gandhian Nationalist "Mass Movement" and its Impact on Indian Christians

Why then, did such deep misconceptions and mistrust develop against Dalit and Tribal mass movements? Why have the Indian mainline churches and theological education in the twentieth century (especially until the emergence of Dalit consciousness and theology from the 1980s) showed distrust of, and trivialized the role of, mass movements in its history? I contend that the development of mistrust and opposition against mass movements had a lot to do with the unfavourable attitude of the national-majority in general and the nationalist leaders in particular towards these movements. Of all the leaders, Mahatma Gandhi, the father of the nation, provides us the best example of such an attitude. We will look at Gandhi's impressions on, and interaction with, Christianity as represented by the missionaries of his time, and his reaction to the issue of conversion. Within this analysis, we will locate his attitude of anti-mass conversion of Dalits to Christianity. The influence of the spirit of nationalism as well as the perpetuation of caste mentality in the church resulted in the strong contempt for mass movements and an internal split of the Christian community into Christians of caste origins and Christians of outcaste (and non-caste tribal) origins. I will presume a basic knowledge of who Mohandas Gandhi, who assumed the coveted and exclusive title "Mahatma" or the great soul, is and what he achieved, and will not relate the heroic story of this great "father of the Indian nation."

Mahatma Gandhi and Christianity

Studies on Gandhi continue to multiply, and in recent years a few have come out on Gandhi and Christianity. Most of the studies on Gandhi's relationship with and views on Christianity are based on analyses of his utterances, speeches and writings related to Christianity as presented to him in his time. These have been collected and published in several forms with some repetitions. Among the collections of Gandhi's writings and statements on Christianity, *Christian Missions: Their Place in India* is the most original and representative piece on the topic. Therefore, we will rely mainly on this collection. Between the contention that he was a secret Christian and the fact that he became the spokesperson against conversion to Christianity, Gandhi's many statements made him appear quite ambiguous. He is, perhaps, the most-quoted figure in the anti-conversion campaign of militant Hindu nationalists in recent years.[26] As Sudhir Chandra has rightly pointed out, those who oppose conversion today in India "exploited the case with which his numerous contradictory utterances on the subject can be selectively cited either way."[27] Rameshwar Shukla 'Pankaj' and Kusumlata Kediya, for instance, declared, "Resurgent Hindutva would force Christianity to be restrained and religious. Gandhiji is our guide in this matter."[28]

Most of the collections of his statements on, and interactions with, Christianity begin with a narrative of his childhood encounter with Christian mission as recounted in his autobiography. While recalling how mutual tolerance among different "branches of Hinduism and sister religions" characterized his home in Rajkot, he said,

> Only Christianity was at the time an exception. I develop[ed] a sort of dislike for it. And for a reason. In those days Christian missionaries used to stand in a corner near the High School and

hold forth, pouring abuse on Hindus and their gods. I could not endure this.... About the same time, I heard of a well-known Hindu having been converted to Christianity. It was the talk of the town that, when he was baptized, he had to eat beef and drink liquor, that he also had to change his clothes, and that henceforth he began to go about in European costume including a hat.[29]

After the autobiography was first published, the authenticity of what Gandhi related here as to what the missionaries used to do was challenged by the Rev. H. R. Scott, the only missionary in Rajkot at the time. Scott denied ever-preaching "in a corner near the High School and pouring abuse on Hindus and their gods" or having any knowledge of a convert who "had to eat beef and drink liquor."[30] Gandhi could not defend his statement and accepted Scott's repudiation, but said that what he had "heard and read since has but confirmed that first impression."[31] Whether Gandhi made up the details of the story or not, this account reflects one strong dimension of Gandhi's opinion on Christianity, namely his dislike of Christianity, especially the form represented by missionaries and British colonial rulers.

Gandhi's interaction with Christianity may be laid out in three stages: his early impression of Christianity and Christian missions in India, his close personal interactions with Christians in London and South Africa during which time he even considered becoming a Christian, and his interaction with Christians, especially missionaries and some converts in India during his national political movement. As we will see, Gandhi's attitude toward Christian missions, especially in connection with conversion, changed gradually and significantly from the first phase of his political movement (1919-1929) to the second (1929-1947). The first impression, though modified and matured in his own way, had a strong influence throughout his life. This early stage, which he later called "beef and beer-bottle Christianity,"[32] found resonance in his criticism of missions, missionaries, and Christian Indians in the later stage.[33] In his own estimation, the most important point in the development of his religious thought was when he came to realize that all religions are equal. He said he came to the conclusion that "all religions were right but every one of them was imperfect" after studying the scriptures of the great religions of the world.[34] He expounded on this by saying,

> If we are imperfect ourselves, religion as conceived by us must also be imperfect. We have not realized religion in its perfection, even as we have not realized God.... And if all faiths outlined by men are imperfect, *the question of comparative merit does not arise.* All faiths constitute a revelation of Truth, but all are imperfect, and liable to error.[35]

Based on this relativistic viewpoint, Gandhi then went on to gather what is good in any religion and discard that which he considered in error in any. What criteria did he use to determine what is right and what is wrong? In one place, he identified truth, non-violence, and reason as the "fundamental maxims" by which he made his determination.[36] In one of his interviews with a Christian thinker, he said, "I exercise my judgment about every scripture, including the Gita. I cannot let a scriptural text supersede my reason."[37] What he considered to be the heart of his religion is moral law, and called it the "Law of Truth." It was on this moral basis that he constructed his greatest political weapon called *satyagraha* (truth-force). Gandhi often came in conflict with others, even with close allies such as Rabindranath Tagore and Jawaharlal Nehru,[38] in what he considered to be right and acceptable. He was often immoderate in taking opposing viewpoints.

It is true that Gandhi, at one point, seriously considered embracing Christianity and claimed to have studied the Bible well. In a number of his writings he narrated his "final deliberate striving to realize Christianity" when he met a well-known and reputed Indian Christian Kali Charan Banerjee in 1901. This meeting led him to state, as a conclusion to his striving to realize Christianity, that "Hinduism, as I know it, entirely satisfies my soul, fills my whole being...."[39] Contrasting his own statement against comparative merits among religions we have quoted above, Gandhi did make comparison between religions and chose what satisfied him, an activity he could not allow others, especially the Dalits, to make. Well-known is his love of the Sermon on the Mount which he compared and somehow tried to unify with Baghavad Gita. In the end, he said, "I find a solace in Bhagavadgita and Upanishad that I miss even in the Sermon on the Mount."[40] As a reformed Hindu (often dubbed "Neo-Hindu") who believed in the plurality of religious conceptions and views under the guise of "toleration" that characterized Hinduism itself, Gandhi had no difficulty drawing from the teachings of Christianity or any other religion and to claim himself to be a follower of Jesus or Muhammad. In addressing missionaries, he in fact challenged them by saying, "If I have read the Bible correctly, I know many men who have never heard the name of Jesus Christ or even rejected the official interpretation of Christianity will, probably, if Jesus came in our midst today in the flesh, be owned by him more than many of us."[41] But he did not regard Jesus as anything more than a great teacher, and vehemently opposed the orthodox Christian claim of moral superiority and its dogmatic basis. To quote his words, "I regard Jesus Christ as one of the greatest teachers of mankind, but I do not consider him to be the 'only son of God.'"[42] In another place, he said, "I rebel against orthodox Christianity" because "it has distorted the message of Jesus Christ."[43] Thus, he rejected orthodox Christianity and its teaching about Jesus. Like one of his great predecessors of Reformed Hinduism, Raja Ram Mohun Roy, he had no difficulty in acclaiming Jesus publicly. But he would not affirm that Jesus was more than one of the greatest teachers. He did not believe that Jesus performed miracles as recorded in the Gospels nor the teaching that Jesus atoned for the sins of the world. There is no doubt that Jesus was "the only begotten son of God" for "the devotees of his generation," wrote Gandhi. "Their belief need not be mine. He affects my life no less because I regard him as one among the many begotten sons of God."[44] Gandhi drew on Hindu pluralism as a basic strength and challenged any claim of superiority over Hinduism.

In a meticulous historical analysis of Gandhi's dialogical interaction with Christians during his political movement in India (1919-1939), John Webster laid out dominant themes chronologically.[45] In the period between 1919 and 1929, Webster identified three themes, all of which came from Gandhi's own agenda. The first of these was Gandhi's criticism of the missionary attitude toward India. Though this theme is dominant during the period, one can see that the theme persisted throughout the 1930s. Side by side with this theme is the next one, namely "Europeanization of Indian converts to Christianity." Denationalization of converts is the other side of the same coin which coloured Gandhi's opinion on Indian converts. The third theme, which steered much of Gandhi's speeches and writings on Christianity throughout his life, and which inspired Hindu fanatics in the years to come, is his objection to religious change or conversion. During the civil disobedient movement (1932) under Gandhi's leadership, Indian Christians' relationship with the nationalist movement greatly improved, but Gandhi's criticism of missionaries and their "proselytizing" work caused great damage to the relationship. In the period following Gandhi's fast-unto-death campaign against the granting of separate electorates to untouchables (Dalits) from 20 September 1932, Gandhi's dialogue with Christians in India was dominated by issues surrounding Dalit conversions (mass movements). Webster's study, as well as most other studies on Gandhi's relationship with Christianity, shows that conversion or religious change became one of the most prevalent themes in Gandhi's criticism of Christianity. We now turn our attention to the issue of conversion and mass conversion in connection with Dalits/Harijans.

Gandhi on Religious "Conversion"

Responding to the question whether missionaries would be welcomed in free (independent) India, Gandhi was quoted by a number of press correspondents as having said:

> If they [missionaries] confine themselves to social and economic uplift they would be [welcome], but if they did as they are now doing, namely using hospitals and schools for the purpose of proselytizing then I should certainly ask them to withdraw. One nation's religion is as good as another nation's. Certainly India's religions are not inadequate for her needs. India needs no spiritual conversion.[46]

The statement, made at the prime of his political career, that is, the early part of 1931, clearly revealed his repugnance to the missionary works on conversion and drew sharp criticisms from Christian leaders, and even from his close Christian friends. Gandhi later explained that the quotation was "a travesty" and a "distorted version of my views." He then offered a revised statement which is not very different from what was reported originally. He said, "Every nation considers its own faith to be as good as that of any other. Certainly the great faiths held by the people of India are adequate for her people. India stands in no need of conversion from one faith to another."[47] Reacting sharply against Gandhi's view expressed in the statement, missionary-evangelist E. Stanley Jones, a friend and a well-known proponent of Gandhi among Christians, distinguished proselytism from conversion and said he also opposed the former. Then he said,

But while I oppose proselytizing I think it is an entirely different thing for me to share my faith with others, and if that sharing leads to moral and spiritual conversion, I believe that person so inwardly converted has a moral right to declare outwardly what he has experienced inwardly and to join any group where that new life might be cultivated.[48]

A simple analysis of Gandhi's statement quoted above reveals several controversial issues. Such issues include treating conversion and proselytism as synonyms; every nation owning its faith or religion; and disallowing Indian citizens the freedom to choose one's own religion or faith. All these do not conform to the secular commitment of the independent India that Gandhi had fiercely fought for. It is not surprising that most intellectual writings by Hindu communal nationalists today utilize Gandhi as a basis for their anti-conversion writings. While Gandhi's dislike of religious change or proselytism is unambiguous, the meanings of his statements are often vague and sometimes they appear to be inconsistent.

One of the difficulties in understanding Gandhi on conversion is his ambiguous use of the term. In one place he said, "I am against conversion, whether it is known as *Suddhi* by Hindus, *Tabligh* by Mussalmans or proselytizing by Christians. Conversion is a heart-process, known only to and by God. It must be left to itself."[49] One notices that when he defines conversion as "a heart-process," it cannot be objected to, but here he also declares, "I am against conversion." Elsewhere, he said "Real conversion springs from the heart and at the prompting of God,"[50] and in another place he declared, "I am ... not against conversion. But I am against the modern methods of it."[51]

Most of Gandhi's strong statements about or against conversion were made in the context of dialogical conversations, some formal and others less formal. Among these, we select two dialogues to analyse his arguments against religious conversion or religious change. The first of these was with A. A. Paul of the Federation of International Fellowships, who asked Gandhi to define his position on conversion. Gandhi, in response, asked Paul to frame definite questions. The following statements were raised on behalf of the Executive Committee of the Madras International Fellowship asking Gandhi to "answer these statements in *Harijan*."

1. Conversion is a change of heart from sin to God. It is the work of God. Sin is separation from God.

2. The Christian believes that Jesus is the fulfilment of God's revelation to mankind, that He is our Saviour from sin, that He alone can bring the sinner to God and thus enable him to live.

3. The Christian, to whom God has become a living reality and power through Christ, regards it as his privilege and duty to speak about Jesus and to proclaim the free offer which He came on earth to make.

4. If any man's heart is so moved by the hearing of this message as to repent and wish to live a new life as a disciple of Jesus, the Christian regards it as right to admit him to the Company of His professed believers which is called the Christian Church.

5. The Christian shall do all in his power to sound the sincerity of conviction in all such cases and shall point out, as he can the consequences of such a step, stressing the duty a man owes to his family.

6. The Christian shall do everything in his power to prevent any motives of self-seeking on his part and of material considerations on the part of the convert.

7. Inasmuch as Jesus came to give full life, and that as a matter of history conversion has often meant an enhancing of personality, the Christian shall not be accused of using material inducements if conversion results in the social uplift of the convert-it always being understood that such shall never be sued as a means to an end.

8. The Christian is right in accepting as his duty the care of the sincere convert, body, soul and mind.

9. It shall not be brought against the Christian that he is using material inducements, when certain facts in Hindu social theory, out of his control, are in themselves an inducement to the Harijan. (But see points 5 and 6).[52]

In his response,[53] Gandhi indicated the complex nature of the statements and dissected them according to his own understanding. As for the first proposition, he said, "if conversion is the work of God, why should that work be taken away from him?" This implies that in his understanding, it was Christian missionaries who were making converts, not the spirit of God. He read this point in isolation and did not relate it to other points. For instance, point 4 directly expresses Christian faith in the possibility of repentance, becoming a disciple of Jesus as a member of the Church. "The second proposition deals with the Christian belief handed to the believer ... the truth of which thousands of Christians born are never called upon to test for themselves..." He concluded that it is dangerous to present such a belief "to those who have been brought up to a different belief." The third proposition, he said, relates to the mystery of religion not understood by common people but only by those who live in the traditional faith.

"The other five propositions [points 4 to 8] deal with the conduct of the missionary among those whom he is seeking to convert," and have no relevance for others. "The last proposition" appalled Gandhi and he calls it "the crown of all the preceding ones … [that] takes one's breath away. For it makes it clear that the other eight are to be applied in all their fullness to the poor Harijans." He clearly asserted his doubt that the Harijans would understand any of these since even "the most intellectual and philosophical persons even in the present generation" are puzzled by "the very first proposition." One can summarize Gandhi's response by saying that all the propositions are based on Christian doctrine and, therefore, had no relevance for others in the first place. They all are too complicated to be understood, especially by Harijans (Dalits) who are the target of the message. While there is some truth in what he said, it is a skilful manner of deflecting and dismissing the arguments. The propositions were addressed to Gandhi and they are logical arguments to make a case against his viewpoint. As the authors explicitly acknowledged, they are Christian viewpoints based on Christian teachings. They were not messages addressed to Harijans or anyone other than Gandhi.

The other conversation on conversion was with his close and most trusted Christian friend, Charles Freer Andrews.[54] "What would you say to a man who after considerable thought and prayer said that he could not have his peace and salvation except by becoming a Christian?" asked Andrews. Gandhi responded, "I would say that, if a non-Christian (say a Hindu) came to a Christian and made that statement, he should ask him to become a good Hindu rather than find goodness in [a] change of religion."[55] Here Gandhi made a skilful change from the question of "peace and salvation" to "goodness." As we have discussed, for Gandhi, moral goodness, not salvation, is the basis of religion. Andrews then said, "I cannot in this go the whole length with you, though you know my position. I discarded the position that there is no salvation except through Christ long ago. But supposing the Oxford Group Movement people changed the life of your son, and he felt like being converted, what would you say?" Gandhi answered, "I would say that the Oxford Group may change the lives of as many as they like, but not their religion. They can draw attention to the best in their respective religions and change their lives by asking them to live according to them…"[56] What is most surprising here is Gandhi's differentiation between one's life and one's religion. He appears to understand religion as a community identity, not as faith-principles for the conduct of lives.

Gandhi's Objection and Criticism of Christian Mass Movements

Many of Gandhi's statements against conversion to Christianity were linked with "mass" conversion of the Dalits (or "Harijans" in his words) to Christianity. One may locate Gandhi's aversion to the Dalits' conversion to Christianity in the context of his conflict with the Dalits' most notorious leader, B. R. Ambedkar, from the early 1930s. We will, however, focus our attention on Gandhi and the Dalit conversion to Christianity. Let me begin the discussion of this topic once again by quoting Gandhi's strong words.

> Presentation, with a view to conversion, of a faith other than one's own, can only be necessarily through an appeal to the intellect or the stomach or both. I do maintain that the vast mass of Harijans, and for that matter Indian humanity, cannot understand the presentation of Christianity, and that generally speaking their conversion wherever it has taken place has not been a spiritual act in any sense of the term. They are conversion for convenience. And I have had overwhelming corroboration of the truth during my frequent and extensive wanderings.[57]

Gandhi's claim of "overwhelming corroboration of the truth" is difficult to verify. No Dalit Christian community or individual, to public knowledge, has reported any interaction with Gandhi on the question of their conversions. So, we do not know how Gandhi corroborated "the truth" here. In *Christian Missions: Their Place in India,* where this 1937 statement of Gandhi was reproduced, it is followed by a collection of disgraceful stories of Christian mission works and conversion of the Harijans, collected and reported by an individual named Thakkar Bapa. There is no denying that missionary activities in India may have included numerous disreputable deeds such as those described by Bapa, and the allegation that economic factors played a role in Dalit conversions is not entirely out of place. However, to claim "the truth" based solely on one's conception of how things can happen—in this case how the presentation of a faith can appeal only "to the intellect or stomach"—is unreasonable and less than persuasive.

The point that Harijans/Dalits cannot understand the presentation of Christianity is the basic tenet of Gandhi, which has been contested strongly by Christians. To illustrate his point, he even likened the Harijans with cows. In the first of his two extensive conversations with John R. Mott, a prominent international leader of Christian missions and ecumenical movement of the early 20th century, Gandhi expressed the uselessness of missionary preaching to the Dalit communities. When Mott asked him why the missionaries should not preach the Gospel to the Dalits, Gandhi answered, "Would you, Dr. Mott, preach the Gospel to a cow? Well some of the untouchables are worse than cows in understanding. I mean they can no more distinguish between the relative merits of Islam and Hinduism and Christianity than a cow...."[58] Shocked by such a comparison, many Christians expressed their dismay and disagreement with Gandhi. Gandhi maintained his position publicly in his article "The Cow and the Harijan."[59] Gandhi's distrust of the Dalits' intellectual ability and reasoning capacity is both absurd and mind-boggling.

As Webster has pointed out, most of Gandhi's attacks on missionaries for their "converting" work among Dalits were made after 1932, the year the Communal Award (for separate electorates for Dalits) was made and Gandhi's fast-unto-death opposition led to the reversal of the Award to Dalits under the well-known "Poona Pact." The Award was based on the argument of Dalit leader B. R. Ambedkar that the Dalits are not Hindus and should be given separate electorates. While Christian leaders like V. S Azariah agreed with Gandhi in opposing the Communal Award for Indian Christians, they vehemently disagreed with Gandhi's aggression against conversion. Gandhi stepped up his attack on conversion of the Dalits apparently in connection with his claim that the Dalits are Hindus. Although Gandhi and Azariah rarely conflicted publicly,[60] Azariah, the missionary-bishop who led thousands of Dalits in today's Andhra Pradesh, was identified as Gandhi's "Enemy Number One" by the Editor of *The Collected Works of Mahatma Gandhi*.[61] Azariah deeply shared Gandhi's nationalist aspirations. In fact, it was in response to Gandhi's request to revoke separate electorates for Christians that Azariah published his second plea to oppose the Communal Award in 1932. But Azariah also opposed Gandhi's rebellious activities such as civil disobedience, non-cooperation and the "Quit India" movements.

Most of Gandhi's written criticisms against the conversions of Dalits came after 1935.[62] Here we should also keep in mind the publication in 1933 of *Christian Mass Movements in India* by J. Waskom Pickett, the outcome of a commissioned study by the National Christian Council of India we have mentioned before. Did Gandhi read this book?[63] He never mentioned the content of the book, but he read about the book in a report on the work and findings of its author published in *The Church Times*, which he severely criticized.[64] The report was on a speech given by J. Waskom Pickett, Bishop of the Methodist Church in India and author of the book in question. Speaking on mass movements in India where "four and a half million of the depressed classes in India" have become Christian, the report quoted him as saying the movement marvelled that "multitudes in India" and hundreds of "high caste people are now coming to the Church." The report concluded with Pickett's declaration that "It is a miracle," "one of the great miracles of Christian history."[65] Gandhi entitled his response "What is a Miracle?" and said, "I have rarely seen so much exaggeration in so little space." Gandhi just could not believe the figure given by Pickett. Unless Pickett included the "conversions due to the movement led by Dr. Ambedkar" to Buddhism, Gandhi thought Pickett must have made an extreme exaggeration. He even offered to correct the figure by saying "He [Pickett] has in mind the figures to date commencing from the establishment of the first church in India hundreds of years ago." What the bishop had done, to Gandhi, was a caricature of a faith by one of its own followers. With a tone of derision, Gandhi exclaimed:

> If all the astounding statements Dr. Pickett has propounded can be substantiated, truly it is 'one of the great miracles of Christian history', nay, of the history of man. But do miracles need an oratorical demonstration? Should we in India miss such a grand miracle? Should we be untouched by it? Miracles are their own demonstration.[66]

The India Conciliation Group (ICG), a group concerned with the deteriorating relations between Gandhi and Christians, worked strenuously to reconcile Gandhi and the Christian leaders. But the effort in the end not only failed, but also, as Susan Billington Harper rightly said, was "counter-productive." The ICG did succeed in arranging a meeting among Gandhi, Azariah, and

Pickett. Because of the promise to keep the content of the meeting confidential, and that the only transcripts recorded by Gandhi's secretary, Mahadev Desai, "disappeared," there is no record surviving. The meeting was soon followed by a controversy as a result of a three-part article written by Donald McGavran where the account of the Gandhi-Azariah-Pickett meeting was reported in detail. At the conclusion of the meeting, according to McGavran, Gandhi said to Azariah:

> You Christians must stop preaching to and making disciples amongst the Depressed Classes. If you do not, we shall make you. We shall appeal to the educated Indian Christians; we shall appeal to your home constituency; and if those fail we shall prohibit by law any change of religion, and we will back up the law by the force of the State.[67]

Both Gandhi and Azariah denied the truth of McGavran's story, and Azariah stated it to be "wholly and absolutely untrue." While the fact that McGavran could report the meeting in such detail is questionable and that the detailed report is clearly deniable,[68] the truth of Gandhi's aggression against conversion to Christianity is undeniable, as he continued to attack the whole phenomenon.

Where does the truth about "mass movements" lie? As mentioned above, as a result of the movements, the number of Christians quadrupled, but not overnight nor in a decade. The comparative figure we have quoted above (1,246,288 in 1872 to 6,020,887 in 1932) reflects the growth (of approximately 4.8 millions) in sixty years' time. If the presentation of Pickett or as it was reported cast the impression that the growth came instantly— and that is how Gandhi appeared to have read it, statistics does not support it. On the other hand, Gandhi's trivialization of the movements and of the transformation of Dalit converts by the Gospel in Indian Christian history is either a major oversight or a political ploy. Azariah clearly opined that it was after seeing the

1931 census report that Gandhi and Rajagopalachari increased their attacks against Christian missionaries and conversion. While Gandhi could hardly believe that such movements had happened, he also condemned Christian missionaries for targeting the Dalits. As we have discussed above, he could not believe that Dalits could experience any genuine spiritual conversion because of their incapacity for reasoning. Someone wrote to inform him that "Lakhs[69] of the Depressed Class people in South India, as you know, have joined Christianity wholesale.... What would you advise about them?" Gandhi wrote,

> In my opinion, they are not examples of real heart conversions. If a person, through fear, compulsion, starvation or for material gain or consideration, goes over to another faith, it is a misnomer to call it conversion. Most cases of mass conversions, of which we have heard so much during the past two years, have been to my mind false coin.[70]

In objecting to the possibility of any "real heart conversion" of the Dalits, Gandhi insisted that every Dalit conversion is being prompted by material gain. While rejecting his take on the former (impossibility of real conversion for Dalits), we agree that non-religious motives played a significant role in the conversion movements. Ironically, one must look at the very Hindu caste-based worldview for the intricate connection between religion, social location, and economic condition/status. There is a strong economic element in the oppressive structure of the caste system and the poverty of Dalits is endemic to their socio-religious identity. The "unbreakable" bounds of the caste people based on the "doctrine" of *karma* (and related to *samsara*) that warrants casteism also shuts out the Dalits (making them "outcastes") from any hope of changing life for the better in one's lifetime except by leaving Hinduism. Leaving Hinduism was the step taken by B. R. Ambedkar in 1936 when he and his fellow Mahar (Dalit) community "left" Hinduism and embraced Buddhism. While Gandhi disagreed with Ambedkar, what Ambedkar and the Mahar community did was a non-issue for Gandhi as he considered Buddhism a part of Hinduism. Ambedkar's conversion, seen to be motivated purely by socio-economic factors, was not endorsed by most Christians even at the time. Bishop Azariah commented, "religion is not a matter that can be adopted or changed by fifty million people at the behest of a leader, however influential he may be. Nor would there be any spiritual gain to the follower from a religion so adopted."[71] The movement surrounding Ambedkar could be seen as a symptom of a larger Dalit revolutionary ferment. Gandhi could neither believe nor allow any revolutionary movement by Dalits, and tried to resolve the Dalit problem as an in-house issue of Hinduism. To this end, he campaigned against untouchability and for the opening of Hindu temples to Dalits, which enjoyed great success. But his strong defence of *varnadharma*[72] (the basis of the Hindu practice of caste system), as his critics including Ambedkar pointed out, could not allow Dalits to be given anything near equal treatment with the rest of Hindu communities. From the Dalit viewpoint supported by many Christians, for any extensive economic change to happen to Dalits as a community, the socio-religious warrant of the oppression in the form of caste had to be removed. In other words, *varnadharma* itself was the root cause of the problem. Unless this root cause is discarded, the only other option is to leave the system and the structure by converting to another religion.

On the issue of the Dalit quest for a fuller life and what role Christians should take, Gandhi clashed with a group of nationalist Christian intellectuals who published a carefully written document entitled "Our Duty to the Depressed and Backward Classes."[73] Acknowledging the revolutionary spirit moving among the Depressed (Dalit) communities, the document unequivocally lauded the political shift in the 1930s (post Communal Award and Poona Pact) to recognize their plight and the steps taken for their increased status by Hindu reformers while also criticizing the tyranny of caste. It encouraged Christians to welcome the new shift in which "the process of absorption of the Depressed and Backward Classes into Hindu community" accompanied by a "great gesture of friendliness" by the Caste Hindus was going on.[74] The document discouraged an "aggressive evangelistic programme" in the current critical situation of the Dalits and even discarded the belief held by many Christians that "the present upheaval is going to result in an influx of the Depressed and Backward classes into the Christian Church."[75] However, it does affirm the "Mass Conversions" of the Depressed and Backward classes in the past as "mainly the outcome of the desire for social justice and all-round uplift" in which "the Christian Church has succeeded in helping large sections of converts from these communities to a higher standard of life ... and to real transformation in the life and character of individuals and groups belonging to these classes."[76] The document closes with two firmly held statements of faith in connection with the Christian role in the uplift of Dalits. The first one says,

> Christianity will continue to exercise the attraction which it has always had for the poor of the land.... Men and women, individually and in family or village groups, will continue to seek the fellowship of the Christian Church. That is the real movement of the Spirit of God. And no power on earth can stem that tide. It will be the duty of Christian Church in India to receive such seekers after truth as it is in Jesus Christ and provide for them instruction and spiritual nurture.[77]

The second affirmation upholds that "the task before the Indian Church is to permeate the ideology and outlook of the land with a genuine respect for the teachings of Jesus and a willingness to accept his leadership in all that concerns personal happiness and national well-being."[78] In reading the document, an outside reader may come away with the thought that this Christian statement may have been greatly influenced by Gandhi's teaching and that Gandhi would acclaim it. Nay, Gandhi strongly repudiated it, and titled his response "An Unfortunate Document." Calling the authors "patronizing," he treated them with deep suspicion and said, "They would not be aggressive for the sake of expedience." Furthermore, "The purpose of the manifesto," he said, "is not to condemn unequivocally the method of converting the illiterate and the ignorant but to assert the right of preaching the Gospel to the millions of Harijans."[79] Would he always be dissatisfied if one did not condemn the conversion of the Dalits? Locating "the key to the manifesto" in the last two points we have quoted above, he said, "these few sentences are a striking instance of how the wish becomes father to the thought."[80] It seems as if any positive or permissive mention of "Mass Conversion", let alone affirmation, pricked his conscience negatively. Who is patronizing in this debate? Cannot one have the liberty to state and profess his or her belief? Did not Gandhi do that even more so?

Concluding Observations

In raising questions regarding Gandhi's thought on religious conversion, especially his objection to the conversion of the Outcastes to Christianity, we are not undermining "the great soul" (or perhaps the greatest soul) of India and his contribution to India. The intention is to investigate the rationale of his objections. What led Gandhi to such a strong objection to conversion? How are we to interpret his antipathy toward Christianity and Christian missions? Gandhi's basic objection to conversion is clear. Because he insisted that all the great religions of the world are equal, there is no point in changing from one to the other. He concluded his response to Paul and the Federation of International Friendship mentioned above by saying,

> I believe that there is no such thing as conversion from one faith to another in the accepted sense of the term. It is a highly personal matter for the individual and his [or her] God.... For I regard all the great religions of the world as true at any rate for the people professing them as mine is true for me.[81]

Gandhi might have thought his statements were quite definite, but when one lays out his various statements, there are serious questions left unresolved. If he insisted that because all religions are equal and there is no "question of comparative merit,"[82] why did he use such comparative language in stating "Why I am a Hindu"? To quote his words,

> Believing as I do in the influence of heredity, being born in a Hindu family, I have remained a Hindu. I should reject it, if I found it inconsistent with my moral sense or my spiritual growth. On examination I have found it to be the most tolerant of all religions known to me.[83]

He then went on listing the qualities of Hinduism. Among the superior quality of Hinduism, he included "its freedom from dogma," its inclusiveness, and that non-violence "has found the highest expression and application in Hinduism" (which includes Jainism and Buddhism). Gandhi gave himself the freedom to examine religions and to make his choice. He gave himself the option "to reject" or to remain in Hinduism, but he could not give the same option to others, especially the depressed classes (or Dalits) whom he called Harijans.

How then do we sum up the contradicting viewpoints between Gandhi and the Christians on conversion, especially of the Dalits? Sudhir Chandra observed that Gandhi carried "the tension between his aversion for and acceptance of conversion"[84]

throughout his life and never "resolved the issue . . . in his mind.
. . . Though the matter was never resolved," he continued,
"Gandhi's argument tended to be more often against than
for conversion."[85] It is important to note that he viewed the
whole issue from the emergent reformed Hindu viewpoint in
the context of the national struggle for freedom and selfhood.
As I have mentioned elsewhere, what American Psychoanalyst
Erik H. Erikson called Gandhi's "dialectic problem" is crucial in
understanding him. To quote Erikson, "[Gandhi] had to call for
a rapid modernization of awareness and aspiration and yet also
to acknowledge and even preserve those aspects of the ancient
social structure which alone could provide irreplaceable elements
of a traditional identity."[86] Traditional and modern, or to use
Clifford Geertz's terms, "primordial" and "civil,"[87] met in Gandhi.
He skilfully utilized (by somewhat modernizing) primordial
sentiments to achieve modern political success.[88] Gandhi's main
goal was to claim Indian "national" self-dignity against colonial
rule, for which he gathered its cultural strength by appealing to
its traditional identity. It is in this context that his critical stance
against western Christianity represented by missionaries and British
colonial rulers has to be located. In the vulnerable political and
cultural condition of his struggle against imperialism, where he
defended Indian selfhood (*Swaraj*) by building its self-sufficiency
(*Swadeshi*) against the impending western cultural eclipsing of its
traditional values, Christian missions in general and Christian
conversion in particular were nothing but menaces for him. From
such a viewpoint, Gandhi looked at the issue of conversion to
Christianity with deep suspicion. This suspicion blinded him from
seeing, *inter alia*, the native initiatives and their importance in
the mass movements, their spiritual genuineness, the Christian
missionary focus on caste Hindus and its ignoring of Dalits, and
the positive impact conversions had realized in the life of the Dalits.

When it comes to Dalit mass conversions in particular, the contradiction between Christian understanding of the movements and Gandhi's is more than a matter of interpretation, but rather is a conceptual contrast. Gandhi's anthropological concept of the "Harijans" looks absurd and unacceptable for Christians. He could not believe that "Harijans" were capable of anything spiritual, and suspected their conversion to be purely the result of material inducement. This contradicts the Christian conception of the human as created by God in his image. On the other hand, Christians claimed to have seen the transformation of Dalit communities as a result of their conversion. While giving him every respect as the nation's "mahatma", Christians have every reason to disagree with him on this issue. One should also recognize that Gandhi's disapproval and denigration of the missionary practice of mission also challenges Christians to be prudent in their understanding of conversion and practice of mission.

Endnotes

[1] See, *inter alia*, Kaj Baago, "The First Independent Movement among Indian Christians," *Indian Church History Review* 1 (1967); George Thomas, *Christian Indians and Indian Nationalism, 1885-1950: An Interpretation in Historical and Theological Perspectives* (Frankfurt am Main et al.: Verlag Peter D. Lang, 1979); D. Arthur Jeyakumar, "Christians and the National Movement in India, 1885-1947," in *Nationalism and Hindutva: A Christian Response*, ed. Mark T. B. Laing (Delhi: ISPCK; Pune: CMS of UBS, 2005), 91-102; Atula Imsong, "Christians and the Indian National Movement: A Historical Perspective," *Indian Journal of Theology* 46 (2004): 99-107.

[2] K. Baago, *A History of the National Christian Council of India: 1914-1964* (Nagpur: National Christian Council, 1965), 29.

[3] An exception is D. Arthur Jeyakumar's study on the Memoranda of 1919, a policy document of the British colonial government on missionaries. Jeyakumar's in-depth study shows how the policy was used against missionaries, especially non-British missionaries who supported the nationalist movement. See D. Arthur Jeyakumar, *Christians and the National Movement: The Memoranda of 1919 and the National Movement with Special Reference to Protestant Christians in Tamil Nadu, 1919-1939* (Calcutta: Punthi Pustak, 1999).

[4] Bipan Chandra and his colleagues describe the nationalist movement for freedom as "perhaps the greatest mass movement in world history." Bipan Chandra, Mridula Mukherjee, and Aditya Mukherjee, *India After Independence 1947-2000* (New Delhi: Penguin Books, 2000), 20.

[5] Because it is the conscious choice of the people so called, we will use the term "Dalit." Because of their use in historical documents, other terms including "untouchables," "outcaste," "Depressed Class," and "Harijans" (the preferred name by Gandhi) will be used interchangeably with Dalit. The term Dalit is derived from Sanskrit root *dal* which means "burst, split, broken or torn asunder, downtrodden, scattered, crushed, destroyed." For a detailed discussion of the term, see James Massey, *Down Trodden: The Struggle of India's Dalits for Identity, Solidarity and Liberation* (Geneva: WCC Publications, 1997), 1-3.

[6] For the use of "*en bloc*", see Duncan B. Forrester, *Caste and Christianity: Attitudes and Policies on Caste of Anglo-Saxon Protestant Missions in India* (London and Dublin: Curzon Press; Atlantic Highlands, NJ (USA): Humanities Press, 1980), 69ff.

[7] John C. B. Webster, *A History of the Dalit Christians in India* (San Francisco: Mellen Research University Press, 1992), 56. The Indian edition of this book is entitled *The Dalit Christians: A History* (New Delhi: ISPCK, 1992, 1996). Hereafter, *Dalit Christians*.

[8] On the life and work of Pickett, see Arthur G. McPhee, *The Road to Delhi: Bishop Pickett Remembered, 1890 – 1981* (Bangalore: SAIACS Press, 2005). The book was originally a Ph.D. dissertation at Asbury Seminary. Unfortunately, all the references to historical sources are eliminated in the published version. For references to the sources, the dissertation may be consulted.

[9] J. Waskom Pickett, *Christian Mass Movements in India: A Study with Recommendations* (Lucknow: Lucknow Publishing House, 1933). The book was published simultaneously in the United States of America by Abingdon Press.

[10] Pickett, 22.

[11] None of the movements among the tribal groups in Northeast India, for instance, show any sign of such "group decision." See my *Ethnic Identity and Christianity: A Socio-Historical and Missiological Study of Christianity in Northeast India* (Frankfurt am Main: Peter Lang, 2002), 141-143 for a discussion on Pickett's and MacGavran's theory in relation to mass conversion in Mizoram. For other parts of Northeast India and other studies, see the chapters by Krickwin C._Marak, J._Puthenpurakal, O._L._Snaitang, A. Wati Longchar, and F. Hrangkhuma in *Christianity in India: Search for Liberation and Identity*, ed. F. Hrangkhuma (Delhi: ISPCK; Pune: CMS, 1998).

[12] See Donald McGavran, "The People Movement Point of View," in *Church Growth and Group Conversion*, 3rd ed. (Lucknow, India: The Lucknow Publishing

House, 1956), 1-7. For McGavran's further works on "Church Growth," see his *Understanding Church Growth* (Grand Rapids: Eerdmans, 1980).

[13] Pickett, 21-23.

[14] Ibid., 9.

[15] Webster, *Dalit Christians*, 71.

[16] Ibid., 315.

[17] Sathianathan Clarke, "Conversion to Christianity in Tamil Nadu: Conscious and Constitutive Community Mobilization Towards a Different Symbolic World Vision," in *Religious Conversion in India: Modes, Motivations and Meanings*, eds. Rowena Robinson and Sathianathan Clarke (New Delhi: Oxford University Press, 2003), 338.

[18] Webster, *Dalit Christians*, 54.

[19] James Massey, "Christianity among the Dalits in North India with special Reference to Punjab," in *Christianity in India: Search for Liberation and Identity*, 1-13.

[20] Pickett, *Christian Mass Movements in India*, 38-52.

[21] Webster, *Dalit Christians*, 52.

[22] See Lalsangkima Pachuau, "Church-Mission Dynamics in Northeast India," *International Bulletin of Missionary Research* 27, No. 4 (October 2003): 154-161.

[23] Webster, *Dalit Christians*, 53.

[24] Cyril B. Firth, *An Introduction to Indian Church History*, Revised (Madras: Christian Literature Society, 1976), 203.

[25] Webster, *Dalit Christians*, 70.

[26] See, *inter alia*, Sita Ram Goel, *History of Hindu-Christian Encounters, AD 304 to 1996* (New Delhi: Voice of India, 1996), and Arun Shourie, *Harvesting our Souls: Missionaries, their design, their claims* (New Delhi: ASA Publications, 2000).

[27] Sudhir Chandra, "Denial of Plurality: Thinking of Conversion through Gandhi," in *Religious Pluralism in South Asia and Europe*, eds. J. Malik and H. Reifield (New Delhi: Oxford University Press, 2005), 184.

[28] Rameshwar Shukla 'Pankaj,' and Kusumlata Kediya, *Gandhiji aur Isaiyat* (Dilli, 2000), quoted in translation from Bipan Chandra, A. Mukherjee, and M. Mukherjee, *India After Independence, 1947-2000*, 184-185.

[29] Quoted from M. Gandhi, *The Story of My Experiment with Truth*, Part I, chapter x.

[30] H. R. Scott, "A Repudiation," in M. K. Gandhi, *Christian Missions: Their Place in India*, ed. Bharatan Kumarappa, second ed. (Ahmedabad: Navajivan Publishing House, 1941, 1957), 5-7; originally published in *Young India*, March 4, 1926.

[31] Ibid., 6.

[32] M. K. Gandhi, *Christian Missions: Their Place in India*, ed. Bharatan Kumarappa, second ed. (Admedabad: Navajivan Publishing House, 1941, 1957), 111. Hereafter, Gandhi, *Christian Missions*.

[33] Here, I beg to disagree with K. L. Seshagiri Rao who opines that Gandhi overcame his earlier resentment of Christianity "when he later on met worthy and noble Christians [in London and in South Africa] and studied the New Testament." See, K. L. Seshagiri Rao, "Mahatma Gandhi and Christianity," in *Neo-Hindu Views of Christianity*, ed. Arvind Sharma (Leiden, New York, København, Köln: E.J. Brill, 1988), 143.

[34] Gandhi, *Christian Missions*, 31.

[35] Ibid., 18, emphasis mine.

[36] Ibid., 112.

[37] Ibid., 151.

[38] See Harold Coward, ed., *Indian Critiques of Gandhi* (Albany, NY: State University of New York Press, 2003).

[39] Gandhi, "An Address to Missionaries," in *Christian Missions*, 30. (The article was originally published in *Young India*, August 6, 1925.

[40] Ibid.

[41] Gandhi, *Christian Missions*, 33.

[42] M. K. Gandhi, *The Message of Jesus Christ*, ed. Anand T. Hingorani (Bombay: Bharatiya Vidya Bhavan, n.d.), 23.

[43] Gandhi, *Christian Missions*, 96.

[44] Ibid., 38-39.

[45] John C. B. Webster, "Gandhi and the Christians: Dialogue in the Nationalist Era," in *Hindu-Christian Dialogue: Perspectives and Encounters*, ed. Harold Coward (Maryknoll, NY: Orbis Books, 1989), 80-99.

[46] Quoted from *Times of India* by E. Stanley Jones in his open letter to Gandhi. "Reports: Two Open Letters to Mr. M. K. Gandhi, 1. Letter from Rev. E. Stanley Jones" *National Christian Council Review* 51, No. 5 (May 1931): 271. See also the quotation from *The Guardian* (April 9, 1931), 158, in Webster, "Gandhi and the Christians," 88.

[47] M. K. Gandhi, "Foreign Missionaries," *Young India* (April 23, 1931), 83. Also see "Mr. Gandhi's Revised Statement," *National Christian Council Review* 51, No. 6 (June 1931): 301-302.

[48] "Reports: Two Open Letters to Mr. M. K. Gandhi, 1. Letter from E. Stanley Jones," *National Christian Council Review* 51, No. 5 (May 1931): 271.

[49] Gandhi, *The Message of Jesus Christ*, 33 (originally published in *Young India*, January 6, 1927).

[50] Gandhi, *Christian Missions*, 84.

[51] Gandhi, *The Message of Jesus Christ*, 34.

[52] Gandhi, *Christian Missions: Their Place in India*, 46-47. Originally published in *Harijan*, September 28 1935.

[53] Ibid., 48-49.

[54] During the question hour in his address to the missionaries in Calcutta in 1925, Gandhi was asked "How ... should the missionaries identify themselves with the masses?" He responded by saying "Copy Charlie Andrews." Such was the depth of trust he had for Andrews. See "An Address to Missionaries," in *Christian Missions*, 35 (originally published in *Young India*, August 6, 1925).

[55] Gandhi, *Christian Missions*, 146.

[56] Ibid.

[57] Ibid., 61, originally published in *Harijan*, June 12, 1937.

[58] Ibid., 175-176.

[59] Ibid., 58-60; originally published in *Harijan*, March 13, 1937.

[60] Gandhi once accused Azariah as offering "baits" to Dalits for conversions. Ibid., 162. Azariah did not respond to this allegation directly except to offer a more general response to Gandhi's criticism of Christian mission.

[61] Susan Billington Harper, *In the Shadow of the Mahatma: Bishop V. S Azariah and the Travails of Christianity in British India* (Grand Rapids, MI: Eerdmans, 2000), 291.

[62] Corroborating the fact that his strong objections to mass conversions came about since 1935,he stated in 1937, "Mass conversions, of which we have heard so much during the past two years ..." (Gandhi, *Christian Missions*, 84). This indicates that he came to learn about them since 1935.

[63] According to Pickett's biographer, Arthur McPhee, the two had met sometime in 1921 when Gandhi visited Arrah in Bihar where Pickett was stationed at the time. See McPhee, *The Road to Delhi*, 142-143.

[64] Gandhi, *Christians Missions*, 53-55, originally published in *Harijan*, December 19, 1936.

[65] Ibid., 54.

[66] Ibid., 54-55.

[67] D. A McGavran, "The Battle for Brotherhood in India Today," *World Dominion* XVI, 3 (July 1938): 261, quoted in Harper, 326.

[68] According to McPhee, Pickett admitted to be the source of McGavran's story. See McPhee, 273.

[69] "Lakh," often used in English in India, means one hundred thousand.

[70] Gandhi, *Christian Missions*, 84, originally published in *Harijan*, September 25, 1937.

[71] "The Bishop Letter," *Dornakal Diocesan Magazine* XII, 12 (December 1935): 3, quoted in Harper, 307.

[72] Gandhi, *Christian Missions*, 116, 28.

[73] The document, as reproduced by Gandhi with his response "An Unfortunate Document," appeared in *Harijan*, April 3, 1937. The reprint in Gandhi, *Christian Missions*, 75-83, is used here.

[74] Ibid., 78-79.

[75] Ibid., 79.

[76] Ibid.

[77] Ibid., 80.

[78] Ibid., 80-81.

[79] Ibid., 82.

[80] Ibid.

[81] Gandhi, *Christian Missions*, 49.

[82] Ibid., 18.

[83] Ibid., 28. "Why I am a Hindu" was originally published in *Young India*, October 20, 1927.

[84] S. Chandra, "Denial of Plurality," 192.

[85] Ibid., 212.

[86] Erik. H. Erikson, *Gandhi's Truth: On the Origins of Militant Nonviolence* (New York and London: W. W. Norton and Company, 1969), 260-01.

[87] Clifford Geertz, *The Interpretation of Cultures* (New York: Basic Books, 1973), 255-310.

[88] See Lalsangkima Pachuau, *Ethnic Identity and Christianity*, 18-19.

CHAPTER 2

Impacts of Nationalism on Christians and Theology in India

Writing optimistically in the early second decade of the twentieth century, an English missionary to India, C. F. Andrews, penned his hope for the growing Indian Church as follows:

> Yet, the evils of the present state of the Church are gradually passing away. They are not inveterate. Both missionaries and congregations have been inspired with a new spirit since the great national revival. The National Missionary Society and other kindred organisations are welcome signs of the change which is leading to self-government and self-support. Life and movement are very much in the air we breathe, and the hearts of Indian Christians are beating with new hopes. The Church in India will soon represent a far more important element in national life than is now apparent, and when the dangers of relapse into idolatry and caste are overcome, she will assimilate as largely as possible the ancient traditions of India, and make them a vital part of her own constructive growth.[1]

Andrews saw the church being inspired by the growing nationalist spirit as she grew out the denationalizing "evils" of the time. He envisioned her to become fully indigenized by assimilating "as largely as possible the ancient traditions of India." Yet, the church in India has been seen as denationalizing through much of the twentieth century. Against the popular notion that Indian Christians have not been patriotic and the church has been denationalizing, there has been Christian narrative about the active participation of some educated Indian Christians in the national movement. There are some important implications to be drawn from this. Yet, in the various forms this narrative has been rehearsed, attention has not been given to the meaning and implications of the narrative. In this chapter, we will try to draw some important meanings and implications of nationalism for the Indian church while acknowledging that only a small minority elite group of Christian participated in the nationalist movement. We will try to show the distinct and broad Christian nationalistic vision of this group, and that the nationalistic ethos of this distinctly Christian vision somewhat preceded the national movement itself and in some respect influenced and fuelled political nationalism. Not only were the Indian Christians leaders patriotic in the broad sense of the term; a representative national ethos of Christians preceded political nationalism in certain ways. Furthermore, we will trace how the nationalist enterprise of a small group of Indian Christian elites helped to give birth to Indian (indigenous) theological thinking. On the other hand, the Indian nationalist movement in the twentieth century has greatly influenced Indian Christian thought. Much of Indian theological development can be seen as responses to Indian nationalist visions. The line of development can be traced through such streams as indigenization, nation-building projects, and dialogical and liberative theologies. Despite such important contributions, one must not forget the fact that the majority Christian population of India had largely remained indifferent to the nationalist movement.

Indian Nationalism and the Christian Missionary Enterprise

The story of Indian nationalism is largely the story of the Indian National Congress, and the story of the Indian National Congress (INC), from the third decade of the twentieth century, is mostly the story of Mahatma Gandhi, which we have described in the previous chapter. The Indian National Congress saw a dramatic change between the first decade (1885 – 1903), and the period that followed, which historians came to call the "extremist phase" (1904 – 1919). Indian Christian participation in the Congress seemed to have followed this change closely. In his study of Christian participation in the Indian National Congress, historian G. A. Oddie showed the rise and decline of Christian participation in the Congress. Between 1887 (two years after the formation of the INC) and 1890, the number of Christians among the delegates of the annual meetings indicated active participation. Of the 607 delegates, 25 were Christians in the annual meeting of 1887. The trend continued until 1890 when there were 22 Christians among the 677 delegates and started declining, especially from the late 1890s. By 1904 (the transitional year to the "extremist phase"), there was only one Christian out of the 1010 delegates.[2] During the first phase when Christians participated enthusiastically, the INC was politically harmless because it served merely as a platform to voice Indian concerns in British India (colonial) government. The dramatic decline appeared to be caused mainly by the fear of extremist politics for independent India without any promise for the safety of Christian community as a small minority group. There may have been other factors, including the death of a prominent Christian leader in the Congress, Kali Charan Banerjee in 1902. C. F. Andrews commented, "If his health had not failed, he would have been elected President of the Congress itself by the votes of Hindus and Muhammadans."[3]

There is no denying that Christians felt safe under British rule and feared persecution by the majority Hindus. In many of the "princely states" of India during British rule, Christian missions were not welcomed and Christianity was derided. In many Indian villages Christians were often the target of communal scorn and persecution. Even by the beginning of the twentieth century, persecution was still common, especially in the villages. Writing in the second decade of the twentieth century, Eugene Stock said that Christian converts of high caste origins continued to suffer persecution individually while Dalit (or Outcaste) Christians suffered as communities. He wrote, "The humblest villagers often have to suffer. Their cattle are stolen, their wells stopped, their neighbours' cows turned into the fields to graze on the springing crops…."[4] Writing in 1908, the words of an Indian Christian by the name of J. J. Ghose clearly explained why the Christians were reluctant to be part of Indian political agitation against the British.

> We do not know in what way it will be of any advantage to Indian Christians if they join the non-Christians in political agitation. If further rights and political privileges are granted to the people of this country, our poor and small community will not have the remotest chance to be profited by them. On the other hand greater powers in the hands of non-Christians may prove dangerous to the very life of our community. We know by experience that wherever the non-Christians are in power the poor Indian Christians labour under great disadvantage and have to suffer humiliation, indignities and even persecution.[5]

In a close-knit Indian village society, social ostracism became a common experience for Christians. Christians lived in fear of the occasional violent outbursts of the Hindu community against them. This fear factor has to be taken into account in considering the historical relation between Christians and nationalist movement in India.

The Indian National Congress experienced a new life when Gandhi began to take the lead from 1919. With his famous non-violent "*satyagraha*" movement against the Rowlatt Act in 1919, and the Non-Cooperation and Khalifat support movements in 1921-22, Gandhi transformed the nationalist movement into a mass movement. While the general populace of India was enthralled by Gandhi's moral command and charismatic leadership, Christians were slower in throwing their entire support. While Gandhi seemed to have gained the respect of most Indian Christians, signs of reservations against his nationalist agenda also appeared among Christians. As discussed in the previous chapter, tension between Gandhi and Christians mounted from the late 1920s when Gandhi increased his attacks on missionaries for their proselytizing works and criticized group conversions of outcastes Dalits ("Harijans") to Christianity. The gap seemed widest when Gandhi criticized "proselytizing" by missionaries and declared that such missionaries would not be welcomed in a free India. While some prominent Christians took their stance, by and large educated Christians eventually caved in to his criticism. By the time India gained independence in 1947, one prominent church leader and theologian Bishop A. J. Appasamy declared, "It is quite necessary to face facts and to recognize that in the fight for independence of India, Christians as a whole had little or no share."[6] Appasamy attributed the main reason to be "the attitude of our missionary teachers."[7] In failing to throw their whole support to the nationalist movement, were the Christians anti-national? Our contention here is that while the majority Christian population, especially in rural India seemed at a quandary and reacted to the movement indifferently, the emerging nationalist ethos captured Indian Christian elites like the rest of the Indians. Yet, most of these educated Christians followed a different trend of nationalistic thought, one that seemed conversant with, and appropriate to, their ecclesiology. While there were few Christians who threw their whole support on the political movement led by Gandhi, most Indian Christian leaders, therefore, maintained critical distance with a certain degree of indifference and developed their own distinct flavour of nationalism. Christian interactions with the Indian nationalist movement was confined to urban elites. One must also recognize the fact that the large majority of Christians were rural folks who were indifferent to the nationalist movement because of their distrust of the caste Hindu leadership. E. C. Bhatty rightly and explicitly stated this point.

> If village Christians and the depressed classes have failed to respond to political propaganda in favour of national solidarity for the attainment purna swaraj, it is due to their distrust and lack of confidence in Indian leaders of high caste origin. The village Christians who comprise 90 per cent of the [Christian] community may be said to be indifferent to the national movement. They are more interested in their emancipation from the socio-economic system. They want social and economic freedom before political freedom.[8]

Rural Christians shared this indifference to the national movement with other depressed class and lower caste communities of the nation.

Whereas political consciousness came to the tribal people much later, thanks to prominent leaders like B. R. Ambedkar, political awareness began among the Dalit people sooner. From the second decade of the twentieth century Dalit communities demanded separate representatives in the constitution-making process. They did not participate in the Rowlatt *Satyagraha* (1919) and Non-Cooperation movement (1920-1922) led by Gandhi.[9] According to Braj Ranjan Mani, "a slow yet steady political awakening" came about among the Dalits in the first two decades of the twentieth century.[10] A memorandum demanding removal of restrictions against them in public schools and in public services was sent to the Governor of Bombay in 1904 on behalf of 15,000 Mahars (a Dalit community). A similar demand was made in 1910 by the Conference of Deccan Mahars. In 1917, the Depressed Classes of Bombay expressly asked the Congress to address the issues of caste oppression and untouchability in exchange for their support, which forced the Congress to commit itself to remove various discriminations.[11] But the Congress' resolution was never translated into action. It was not until Gandhi was forced to negotiate with the Dalit leaders that the issue of caste oppression against the Dalits was given due attention. The Dalits had their representatives at the First Round Table of Conference of 1930-31 in the persons of S. Srinivasan of Madras and B. R. Ambedkar of Bombay; the latter became one of India's foremost scholars and a Dalit leader.[12] Gandhi did not attend the First Round Table, but attended the Second conference in 1931, where, in the words of Eleanor Zelliot, "a clash of beliefs about the solution for the problem of untouchability led to long-lasting difference between Gandhi and Ambedkar."[13] The Government awarded separate electorates to the Dalits later the same year. In opposition both to the Dalit separate electorates and the Hindu practice of regarding the Dalits as polluted and untouchables, Gandhi did a fast-unto-death protest. It resulted in a negotiated compromise called the Poona Pact by which Ambedkar agreed to surrender separate electorates, and in its stead received several seats reserved for Dalits. In all these, the Dalit Christians, which comprised the majority of Indian Christians at the time, stood uneasily as Christians.

Indian Christian Nationalist Ethos

Nationalistic consciousness in the form of indigenizing Christian identity and the church began to take shape among Indian

Christians quite early. Even before the formation of the Indian National Congress in 1885, some educated Indian Christians expressed their yearning for the national identity of their Christian faith. Protestant Christians in different parts of India formed regional associations across denominational lines and banded together under their common "native" identities. Three non-denominational associations in different parts of India emerged as the main representatives of this phenomenon. These were the Bengal Christian Association, the Western India Native Christian Alliance, and the Madras Native Christian Association.[14] As D. V. Singh has pointed out, these associations were expressions of "the search for [national] identity"[15] and they paved the way for nationalist thinking. The earliest of these associations, the Bengal Christian Association[16] was formed in 1868-69. Two well-known Christian leaders and thinkers, Kali Charan Banerjee and Rev. Lal Behari Dey, led the association. It was this association and its leadership that inspired Surendranath Banerjea to launch the Indian Association of Calcutta, which led one of the first movements for political independence of India.[17]

Indian Christian leaders and thinkers expressed their longing for integrating Christianity with the cultural identity of the nation through several non-denominational churches they founded or proposed. In 1858, a group of Christians left mission churches and formed "the Hindu Church of the Lord Jesus" in Tinnevelly (Tamil Nadu) of South India. This was perhaps the first organized Church of distinctly indigenous nature in India.[18] Along the same line as this new church, Rev. Lal Behari Dey of Bengal, who had demanded equality between Indian ordained ministers and foreign missionaries as early as the 1850s, proposed a "National Church of Bengal" in a paper he presented at the Bengal Association meeting in 1869-70.[19] The proposed Church was to be non-denominational, comprising all Indian Christians, and would have

only the Apostolic Creed as its confessional standard.[20] Although
suppressed by the missionaries, it influenced the formation of
similar ideas in the future. Other members of the Bengal Christian
Association, namely K. C. Banerjee and Joy Govinda Shome
came to strongly identify with Indian nationality when they
formed *the Calcutta Christo Samaj* in 1887. The two founded a
newspaper, *The Bengal Christian Herald* in 1870 in which they
freely expressed their views. A quotation from the first issue of
the paper is representative of their view:

> In having become Christians, we have not ceased to be Hindus.
> We are Hindu Christians, as thoroughly Hindu as Christians.
> We have embraced Christianity, but we have not discarded our
> nationality. We are as intensely national as any of our brethren
> of the native press can be.[21]

They were clear in their teaching to indigenize Christianity in
India. In his lecture to missionaries in 1888, Banerjee strongly
held missionaries responsible for making Christianity a foreign
religion in India. He said that the missionaries "should become
Hindus" just as St. Paul became all things to all people.[22]

Quite similar in intent and nature to the *Christo Samaj*
of Calcutta was the National Church of Madras founded in
September of 1886 by a medical doctor, S. Parani Andy. Both
functioned as non-denomination churches where baptisms and
even ordinations were performed. Like the *Christo Samaj*, the
National Church was also heavily influenced and inspired by
a Hindu reformed organization called the *Brahmo Samaj*. One
should also remember that these were founded around the same
time as the Indian National Congress and they went further in
expressing nationalist feelings than the latter. Although little is
known about the pattern of worship and other activities, these
two churches clearly expressed the nationalist ideal of an Indian
church during the height of the modern missionary movement

in India. Membership of the *Christo Samaj* soon dwindled and the church was dissolved by 1894. The National Church grew strong at the beginning of the twentieth century, but it was never a large church. It became part of the Church of South India in 1948. A historian of Indian Christianity, Kaj Baago, identified the missionaries' fear of splitting the Indian church and the native Christian dependency on foreign mission resources as the main reasons of the failures.[23] Here we should also note that both churches as well as other efforts to indigenize Indian Christianity were all the works of educated elite groups largely as a protest against missionary domination. The efforts were confined to the urban elite Christians and the movement they created did not reach the mass of indigenous rural Christians at any time.

Christian Nationalists during the Nationalist Movement

Can we talk of Christian nationalists in the history of India? Can there be such a thing as Indian Christian nationalism? In an effort to identify Christian roles in the nationalist movement and thoughts, George Thomas interprets Christians to be part and parcel of Indian nationalism and calls them "Christian Indians" putting the emphasis on the Indian identity and uses Christian as a simple qualifier.[24] While this may be conceptually plausible, the theological appropriateness and historicity may be questioned. He idealized "Indian Christianity Movement" as Indian Christian nationalism, which he clearly contrasted to "organized ecclesiastical bodies" which did not support Indian freedom movement.[25] Historically, while a few may be categorized as Christian Indians, there were church leaders who appeared to be as nationalist as anyone else but who maintained their Christian distinctiveness as their point of departure. For Christians, there is a doctrinal call to be prophetic and, thus, to maintain critical distance. As M. M. Thomas made clear in his writings in the 1940s and 1950s,[26]

Christians should maintain critical distance especially because nationalism has the potential of turning idolatrous.[27] As we will see, the larger group of Christians represented for our analysis by K. T. Paul and V. S. Azariah upheld a position that was different from mainstream political nationalism, although they rightly maintained that they were nationalistic.

During the "extremist" phase of the Indian National Congress when most Christians withdrew their support of the Indian National Congress, the lone Christian voice was that of Brahmabandhab Upadhyaya for the national freedom of India. A journalist-theologian, a Christian *sannyasin,* and an activist for the independence of India, Upadhyaya came to adopt Vedanta philosophy as the basis for understanding Christianity in India. As "the first Indian Christian theologian to enter into a positive dialogue with the indigenous theological and philosophical tradition of Hinduism,"[28] Upadhyaya pioneered the effort to reconcile Christianity with Indian culture, tradition, and nationality. His identification with the indigenous culture of India and the struggle against western political and cultural domination led him to distance himself gradually from the Church. The last seven years of his life (1900-1907) was heavily occupied with his advocacy of Indian national freedom. Robin Boyd wrote, "Outside Christian circles most Indians today remember him chiefly as a patriot, one of the first, if not the first to have advocated complete political independence for India."[29] Political advocacy for Indian independence was one of the factors that strained his relationship with the church. There were a few others who seemed to have severed their ties with the church because of their support for nationalist political movement. The works of Christian Gandhian such as S. K. George from the 1930s until his death in 1960 is one prime example.[30] While not involved as a Christian leader, V.

Chakkarai, who later became a well-known Christian thinker, was among those who joined Gandhian non-cooperation movement.[31]

While these few supporters did so by way of protesting the Christian attitude of aloofness and severing themselves from the church, support for the nationalist movement grew from within the Christian community through some noted leaders. Among those who relate the question of Indian national identity and Christian teachings were a few educated laymen. M. M. Thomas listed four names. They are: C. F. Andrews, S. K. Rudra, S. K. Datta, and K. T. Paul. Andrew's thoughts are expressed in *The Ideal of Indian Nationality*, and *The Renaissance in India*; Rudra's in *Christ and Modern India*; and Paul's in *The British Connection with India*.[32] Rudra and Andrews were close associates who lent their hands of utmost support to Gandhi. In fact, prompted by Rudra, Andrews went to South Africa with W. W. Pearson to persuade Gandhi to come home to India and shift his political goal for India.[33] S. K. Rudra's son Ajit Rudra is quoted as complaining, "No one seems to recognize that Gandhi lived as my father's guest off and on for nine years."[34] Gandhi himself had testified that his "Non-cooperation [movement] was conceived and hatched under his [S. K. Rudra's] hospitable roof."[35] Yet, this is not to say that Rudra uncritically threw himself to Gandhi's political movement.

Beyond the strong nationalist tendencies which were apparent among these few Christian leaders, the educated class of Christians was quite influenced by the nationalist movement. In 1919, leaders of the National Missionary Council made a statement saying, "during the past ten years [any close observer] cannot fail to have become aware of the growing dissatisfaction with what is generally known as mission service and of the extreme difficulty of persuading men of good education to enter the ministry of the Church or to identify wholeheartedly with its activities."[36] This observation led to "a small informal conference between some of these men and a few European missionaries" in April 1919 in Allahabad.[37] The findings of the conference admitted to "the growing tension in India between foreign missions and the Indian Church," and said, "A growing sensitiveness to the divergence of national ideals and an increasing reaction against all things of foreign origin is an inevitable outcome of the growth of national consciousness."[38] This was an eye-opener for the missionaries as they came to realize the growing national consciousness among young and educated Indian Christians. As stated above, we do not yet see many Christians throwing their unconditional support for the political nationalist movement led by Gandhi, but national consciousness clearly gained strength among the Christians. The majority of Indian Christians seemed to empathize quite strongly with the nationalist movement, but did not identify with the movement unreservedly. They seemed to be torn between their national (Indian) and religious (Christian) fraternities.

The tension within the Christian community as well as among individual Christians is illustrated well by the responses of Christian institutions to Gandhi's non-cooperation movement in North India. Gandhi conceived the plan of the non-cooperation movement while staying in the house of S. K. Rudra, an Indian Christian leader who was the Principal of St. Stephen's College in Delhi. But Gandhi could not convince Rudra and the students in Delhi colleges to join the movement, especially as the call involved boycotting government-aided educational institutions.[39] Rudra praised Gandhi's non-cooperation movement as "a mighty spiritual call to righteousness, both in public and private, social and business life of the people, with an implicit childlike faith in God who wants righteousness to flourish upon the earth."[40] Although not joining the movement as an institution, Forman

Christian College in Punjab lost 156 students during the "non-cooperation" agitation.[41]

A glimpse of Indian Christian thought on nationalism may be gained by analysing some representative Christian leaders' responses. For this purpose, K. T. Paul and V. S. Azariah are good representative thinkers for their active engagement with the life of the Christian community and their outspokenness on nationalist issues. Together with fourteen other Indian Christian leaders,[42] the two founded the National Missionary Society (NMS) in 1905 which, as the name indicates, was a strong effort to nationalize mission and Christianity in India. Although "slow" in "process", according to Donald Fossett Ebright, the society did develop indigenous missions in various and remarkable ways.[43] The two leaders of the NMS, K. T. Paul and V. S. Azariah made distinguished contributions in nationalizing Indian Christianity and Christianizing Indian nationality. Among the two, Paul appears to have done more in this respect as a lay leader who was relatively freer from the clutches of church administrations. If Paul, as a popular national YMCA leader, was better in understanding the aspirations of educated Indians, as a missionary-bishop in rural India, Azariah was closely related with the general Christian populace and better understood their plights and dreams.

Both Paul and Azariah, though clearly disagreeing with Gandhi's position of equality of all religions with their faith in the superiority of Christian faith, claimed to be as nationalist as any other members of the Congress. Their nationalist stance was always within their faith in the catholicity (or universal validity and claim) of the Gospel. Through their leadership positions, they helped to promote nationalism within the Christian community. Because of their Christian identity, they were often ostracized as unpatriotic and criticized for not being members of the Indian National Congress. In response, Azariah once exclaimed,

> My love to my countrymen and my nationalism—they [the critics] think—ought to be measured by my attitude to Congress or to political problems. No, I say my love to my country may be exercised through my ex-political work. If I labour to remove illiteracy, dirt, social enslavement and superstition of the neglected and the unprivileged or underprivileged—am I to be reckoned a foreigner with foreign sympathies with no love for my country? Should I be denounced as unpatriotic, simply because I am not dressed in a particular way or do not eat in a particular style or am not a member of a political party?[44]

In his book *India and the Christian Movement* (earlier published as *India and Missions*) which was written for Christian readership, Azariah identified four major problems facing Indian Christians. One of these is "The problems of civic relationships." In this, he urged Indian Christians to be involved in building a new India. He wrote,

> [E]very Indian Christian is a citizen of India and every man and woman must contribute his or her share in the creation of new India. We have a duty to God and to our Saviour; we have also a duty to our country and our countrymen. And that duty is not discharged merely by preaching the Gospel to all. The Christian with a new vision of service and high ideals of social conduct must be at the forefront of all movements for the betterment of society and for the amelioration of conditions that make life miserable for our fellow countrymen.[45]

As shown earlier, although strong tension existed between Gandhi and Azariah on issues surrounding religious conversion which they could not settle even after meeting in person, they showed mutual respect and both acknowledged their place in the service of Indian nationality and nationhood. Azariah agreed with Gandhi on the latter's stance against a Christian communal electorate and, at the request of Gandhi, strongly urged the Christian community to vote against it.

K. T. Paul, who died on April 11, 1931, at the young age of 55, had the chance to know only the period before 1931. Gandhi's works and thoughts, especially the indigenizing and ethical forces, left a major mark in him. The first major strike against the British rule under Gandhi's leadership came about in the years 1921 and 1922 as a combination of the non-cooperation movement and the support for the Khilafat movement. Commenting on Gandhi's solidification of the nationalist movement in this period, Paul wrote, "The magnetic personality of Mr. Gandhi fused the comrades into a willing solidarity which gave to the whole National Movement an altogether fresh vision of high purpose and noble possibility, higher and nobler than had ever been realized before."[46] To Paul, the "implanting of 'ethical purpose' into the very core of the National Movement is an achievement of Mr. Gandhi."[47] He introduced his book *The British Connection with India* (written between 1924 and 1926) with the common question he encountered during his trip in England in 1924, "What does India want?" He responded this question with the answer "India wants *Swarajya*" (or home rule) with a qualifying statement that this answer is "accurate but far from satisfactory" because of the complex meaning of the phrase.[48] While Gandhi left such a significant impression on him, Paul did not wholly approve of Gandhi's *Satyagraha* and non-cooperation movements.[49] Had he faced Gandhi after 1931, when Gandhi gradually turned rigorously critical of religious conversion, especially of the Dalits, like many other Christian leaders, Paul might have grown critical toward Gandhi.

After Gandhi was imprisoned in 1922 and subsequently retreated from political activities for the next seven years (until

1929), the main works of Gandhi Paul knew were those of non-cooperation and Khalifat movements of 1921-22, and the early part of the Civil Disobedience movement beginning in 1930. Paul's inclination toward nationalism was not to be credited mainly to Gandhi. In fact, his nationalistic zeal was clearly evident before he was exposed to Gandhi's influence. He started writing about nationalism and Christians as early as 1909.[50] In his revealingly-titled article of 1919, "How Missions Denationalize Indians," Paul bemoaned the denationalizing outcomes of Christian missions in India and criticized the attitude of the missionaries who produced them. He wrote, "The first missionaries, of whatever sect, inculcated a holy horror of those things which express the spirit of India."[51] Indian Christianity, for Paul, should be enriched wholly by the rich folklore of India, its distinctive music and community values. "India has expressed her genius in certain lines in the religion and life of her children of which her Christians may well be proud."[52] K. T. Paul was invited by the Viceroy to represent the Indian Christian community in the First Round Table Conference in November-December of 1931. In his speech at the conference, Paul strongly identified Indian Christian community with the national community and took the stance common to all parties. He stated, "We crave for our India a real place, not merely in the British Commonwealth, but also in the sisterhood of all nations, a place that is real and effective for the good of the entire world."[53]

As the stories of both Azariah and Paul show, the Indian Christian support of the nationalist movement had grown quite considerably during the decade of the 1920s. While most Christians seemed to have issues with some methods employed by the Congress, they became more and more vocal in expressing their nationalist stance. An example is a message and an appeal for a Round Table Conference issued in 1930 by a group (signatories) of 65 Indian and British Christians. The statement reads:

We have no hesitation in associating ourselves with the aspirations of India to achieve an equal and honourable place in the family of nations…. We are deeply distressed by the increasing spirit of distrust and bitterness between Britain and India, as revealed in the present struggle.

The time calls for a spirit of magnanimity and acts of conciliation on all sides, without which, the purpose of all who are seeking India's highest welfare cannot be achieved. Believing strongly that the only lasting solution will be reached through frank discussion in the spirit of mutual trust and sympathy, we express the earnest hope that there may be held a Round Table Conference which will be truly representative of all parties and interests….[54]

The message clearly shows the independent stance from the political parties taken by the group while supporting the creation of India as a nation-state. It shows their trust in all the parties' genuineness of the longing for India's welfare, including the British Raj. The statement seems to represent the position of the Indian Christian majority in the 1930s. If one is to identify a major factor that distinguished Indian Christian national ethos from that of the political nationalist movement, it would be the relatively positive attitude toward, or higher ability to trust, the British ruler as the above quotation shows. This is not to say that there was a clear-cut position between Christians and non-Christians in their response to western cultural forces. As much as there have been various responses and reactions to western civilization among Hindu communities,[55] the Christians of India also differed among themselves. While the mass of rural Christians was indifferent to the nationalist freedom movement, there were a few, as mentioned above, who fit well with George Thomas's description of "Christian Indians" who clearly chose to prioritize their national Indian identity. The rest of the urban educated Christians seemed to have existed in tension between their national identity and their Christian identity. What John Webster said about "the educated urban Christian elite" in north-west India in the early 1920s seem to be true to most other regions even in the subsequent decade, namely that they were "drawn towards the nationalist cause, albeit in its moderate form and with some reservations...."[56]

As mentioned earlier, the vast majority of Christians were rural Christians for whom nationalism was secondary to their immediate socio-economic need. They may have had lesser trust in the majority's movement for freedom as their own freedom. Both Christian and non-Christian depressed classes looked for a different or additional freedom than the national majority's political freedom. The voice of the Dalits as represented by B. R. Ambedkar was clearly against Gandhi's. The rural Christian disposition may be located somewhere between Ambedkar and the elite Christian voice represented by K. T. Paul. Even as most Indian Christians showed their reservations against the political movement for independence, the nationalist movement also had a deep influence on Christianity in India. The impact of the Indian nationalist movement on Christian thought on its missional identity can be traced historically through the development of indigenization of Christianity for the creation of indigenous theology and Christian community.

Developing Theology in the Nationalist and Post-Independent Eras

Writing in the mid 1960s, an Indian thinker and church leader, D. G. Moses, exclaimed over the dramatic changes of the time:

> The winds of change are blowing nowhere more fiercely than in the theological world. Concepts which were once regarded as fundamental are relegated to a place of secondary importance and categories that were considered as marginal become central and determinative.[57]

In India, the 1960s saw the height of the nationalist approach in theology. By this time, even those thoughts such as those of

Brahmabandhab Upadhyaya and the Madras-based Christian "Rethinking Group" had received due attention and wide approval. Until it was supplemented by such other approaches as the liberational "subaltern" approach and postcolonial theories, indigenous nationalist theology dominated the scene. Among non-European nations, India has one of the longest continuing histories of theological engagement.

How did this nationalistic theological approach come about? How has the developing national ethos affected Indian Christianity and its theological and missionary thinking? At least three general lines of development emerged. The first of these is a consideration of Indian Christian identification with the nation through (a) indigenizing Christianity and the Christian message, and (b) Christians in secular India and their missional participation in the nation-building project of India. Secondly, the Christian consideration of its encounters with Hindus and Hinduism through various means as theological identification, dialogical interaction, and evangelistic witness is to be seen as positive Christian response to the nationalist ethos. This line of development has yielded rich theological works. The third line of development that must be given due consideration is the emergence and work of indigenous missionary agencies in India. In the remainder of this chapter, we deal with the first point, and in the next chapter, we pick up the third point. The second point is one that has received wide attention and numerous works have come out. We will, therefore, skip the topic in the present work. While much of what we discuss here is theological in nature, our interest is in its historical development.

Indigenization of Christianity as Identification with the Nation

The history of Christian indigenization in India can be traced along two separate lines. The first of these is from the missionary principle of creating an indigenous church as propounded by Henry Venn and Rufus Anderson from the middle of the nineteenth century. The missionary goal, according to this proposition, is to form an indigenous church characterized by three selves, namely self-supporting, self-governing, and self-propagating. This proposition was further developed by others such as John Nevius, D. J. Flemming and Roland Allen as missionary practice and thoughts, and their impact reverberates in various ways and forms even to this day. Immanuel David pointed out that this form of indigenization is "structural" in nature and distinct from cultural and socio-political indigenization.[58] But structural indigenization has cultural foundations and applications, and cannot be wholly distinguished. Without socio-cultural supports, structural changes would hardly succeed.

Quite apart from this line of missionary discussions was the development of indigenous Indian theological reflections. Some Indian indigenous theological works, such as that of Krishna Mohun Banerjee,[59] came about around the same time as the missionary principle of indigenous church took shape. The two streams seem to have merged sometime during the third decade of the twentieth century among Protestant Christians in India. As the church's project, it was in connection with the change of the National Missionary Council to the National Christian Council of India, Burma and Ceylon in 1923 that the theme of indigenization was taken up.[60] Of special interest in the early years of Indian theological reflections was the participation of non-Christian Hindus (often grouped as Neo-Hindus) in the theological reflections and constructions. Led at first by the Reformed Hindu group we have mentioned before, the *Brahmo Samaj*, such theological reflections and interactions continued up to the nationalist movement. They were closely linked with the pioneer Christian nationalist thinkers such as Brahmabandhab Upadhaya. After Upadhaya, a new generation of indigenous thinkers emerged. A scholar-turned-church-leader, A. J. Appasamy, wrote several books that creatively connect Christianity with the Hindu religious system. Chief among them are *Christianity as Bhakti Marga* and *The Gospel and India's Heritage*. Like Upadhyaya, Appasamy was occupied with the need to make the Christian message meaningful to Hindus. But while Upadhyaya appealed to Sankara's *advaita Vedanta* philosophy as the basis to interpret Christian message, Appasamy used Ramanuja's *visasdvaita* and the *bhakti* tradition, which appeals to the mystical dimension of Hinduism. Appasamy pleaded that Christians should preach from within Hinduism and not without. He said, "Feeling with them their intense feelings, sharing with them their deepest longings, thinking with them through their most baffling problems, following them in their highest ideals; doing all these in that measure and to that degree which our loyalty to Christ permits."[61]

Quite close in their thinking to Appasamy were members of a group of thinkers, most of whom were laymen based in South India in the first half of the twentieth century, often referred to as "the Rethinking Group." The group's name was derived from the title of the book the group co-authored *Rethinking Christianity in India*.[62] The group consisted of V. Chakkarai, P. Chenchiah, A. N. Sudarisanam, Eddy Asirvatham, S. Jesudasan, G. V. Job, D. M. Devasahayam, and A. K. Sharma.[63] Among them, Chakkarai and Chenchiah became significant theological contributors through their creative interweaving of Christianity and Indian cultural and philosophical systems. In their *Rethinking*

Christianity in India volume, the group demanded that "the Indian church should think and act for itself and make Christianity an indigenous movement."[64] As an indigenous entity, Christianity in India "should assume an Indian expression in life, thought, and activity.'"[65] The group related Christianity closely with the Hindu religio-cultural and philosophical systems and critiqued Christian fear to identify with the nation and the nationalism movement of the time.[66] Christocentric Chakkarai proposed having "the religious genius of India" form "the precondition of Christ and his *avatar*", replacing the Jewish religious and cultural background of the New Testament.[67] The incarnate Christ, said Chakkarai, is the face of God for the human. The controversial and often provocative Chenchiah confessedly regarded "the supreme value of Christ" without relinquishing his Hindu heritage which is "his spiritual mother."[68] Seeking what he calls "the raw fact of Christ," Chenchiah did not have a particularly high regard for the apostles. While Chakkarai regards the incarnation (*avatara*) of Christ as the point of theological departure, Chenchiah saw Christ not as "fully God and fully human", but as "the new Man", one in between God and human. Appasamy we have discussed above; Chakkarai and Chenchiah were considered too radical by many, such that in publishing the books of Appasamy and Chakkarai, the publisher Christian Literature Society was criticized and was forced to write prefatory notes when a study on these three theologians was published the next time. The notes explain that the publisher was not responsible for the opinion but encouraged the "experimental thinking" of these theologians.[69]

Attempts to construct viable Indian theological reflections within the mainstream church cast quite a different picture from the radical rethinking group. The first Indian Theological Conference for Protestant churches and theological institutions was held in 1942 in Pune, Maharashtra. The finding described the unity of conviction in the conference "that the essential content of the Christian Faith is the same for all times, places and circumstances, but that in different times, places and circumstances, the expression, interpretation and application must both grow out of and meet the actual situation...." The conference understood theology quite narrowly and took up indigenization or "Indianisation" in a cautious manner. The report distinguished "dogma" as the essential content and "the absolute element" of theology from "doctrine" as "the relative element" which expresses, interpret, and applies theology. [70] In its task "to explicate doctrine," the report said that "we would stress our opinion that the 'Indianisation' of Christianity refers only to such changes in external forms and terms as will make the unchanging Gospel intelligible in India." [71] Compared to the rethinking group, the stance of the conference was narrow and conservative, yet saw the study of "Indian non-Christian religious thought" [72] to be an essential theological task. The 1940s saw wide self-assessment of Indian Christians at the national level in the light of challenges posed by the nationalist movement. Interest in indigenization and nationalization of the Church spurred great interest. Summarizing the writings on the theme of indigenization in the *National Christian Council Review* during the decade, U. Meyer found "three main *stimuli* for the quest for indigenization." They are: (1) the felt-need to present the Gospel intelligibly in the language and thought form of the people, and (2) the desire to free the Indian church from dependency on foreign funding and personnel. For leaders like V. S. Azariah, this is a spiritual issue. G. V. Job, a Rethinking group member, proposed a revolutionary withdrawal of the resources where Indian Churches will "sink or swim." Meyer's final stimulus was (3) the charge by non-Christians that they (Christians) are not patriotic and that Christianity is a foreign religion. The voices calling for indigenization multiplied, but the discussions and reflections are those of the educated and progressive Christians while the majority of Christians needed to be reached with the idea and helped in applying them. The discussions did not neglect this, and the call for spiritual revival and sacrificial life was loud and clear.

One of the most important steps resulting from this indigenizing effort was the Christian ashram movement. Although a different form of Christian ashram had been practiced by the great poet Narayan Vaman Tilak before the emergence of Gandhi as the leader of the nationalist movement, as Helen Ralston rightly said, the Christian ashram movement came about under the influence of the nationalist movement.[73] For most of the early Christian ashrams such as Christukula, Christa Prema Seva Sangh, and Sat tal, Mahatma Gandhi and his *Satyagraha* ashram in Sabarmati (near Ahmedabad, Gujarat) was the inspiration and the model. The challenge of Gandhi on sacrificial life and active service of love greatly inspired Christian ashram leaders and founders. For Christians, the ashram model was expected to become a tool for theological and ministerial formation,[74] and for missional witness.[75] The ashram as missionary practice was introduced and popularized within the National Missionary Society circle.[76] Along with the ashram movement was the effort to indigenize Christian worship in the cultural context of India. Ashrams seem to have made progress in this aspect while the general Christian population in the church lagged behind considerably. Adoption of Indian music and songs is the exception rather than the rule even to this day. The Catholic Church came to adopt the Ashram style and concept later after Vatican II in the 1960s.

The 1950s saw new issues surrounding missionary status in independent India. Churches in many parts of India were funded by foreign support and the dependency syndrome was prevalent. While leaders and thinkers of Indian Christians made efforts to identify the church with the nation by indigenizing it, an anti-Christian and anti-missionary movement was also brewing strongly in India. The new missionary visa policy of 1955 and its stricter implementation in the 1960s were part of the anti-missionary spirit of the day. This new policy, which will be discussed in the next chapter, gradually eliminated foreign missionaries from India and forced Indian churches to either "sink or swim." While most churches in the South and Northeast have been swimming quite smoothly, in other regions, many churches struggled. As discussed above, the missionary policy of devolution as a part of the indigenization process involved making the church self-supporting and self-governing.

Secularism, Nation-Building, and Indian Theology in the Independent India

The ongoing effort of Indian Christian identification with the nation took a turn in the mid 1950s from one of indigenization to what we may broadly call "dialogue" with the secular and religious aspects of the nation. By the early 1960s, the issue of indigenization as a protest against Christian identification with western culture was considered by some Indian theologians to be completed. M. M. Thomas declared, "Indigenization is an over-worked topic …. There were days when Christianity was identified too uncritically with western culture; the cry for indigenization was then a protest against this identification."[77] Not all theologians agreed with Thomas' assessment, but he was among the new generation of thinkers who set what Russell Chandran calls "New Trends in Indian Theology." The trendsetters really were those associating with the newly reorganized Christian Institute for the Study of Religion and Society (CISRS) led by Paul D. Devanandan and M. M. Thomas. Devanandan and Thomas redirected Indian theology to identify with the national life, issues, and problems as it sought to build itself into a new nation. Instead of focusing the attention on particular Christian issues related to the nations, they pushed the Christians to address issues the nation faced as citizens of the nation but from a distinct Christian viewpoint. Originally the gluing factor of this new trend of thought was the project which came to be called "Christian Participation in Nation-Building." The project sought:

(1) to work out the elements of a Christian understanding of certain crucial issues in the political, economic and social development of modern India;

(2) to enter into conversation with socially-conscious non-Christians, both secularist and Hindu, in order to consider together the nature of an adequate social philosophy for the new India, and to work out the basis of Christian co-operation with them in social action.

(3) to help the church in India to rethink the pattern of her life, mission and service and to reorient her policies and programmes accordingly, with relevance to her call to social witness in a developing nation.[78]

We quote this at length because it represented both the core of the new trend and the understanding of Christian mission that came to re-write much of Indian Christian theological thought within the Indian Church.

The group surrounding the study project sought dialogues with secular and non-Christian Indians on various national issues. In addition to their own contributions through writings, they organized consultations on various national and regional issues, and engaged in long-term studies of selected themes. The study project itself was comprised of consultation, a working party of writings, and a symposium of Christian and non-Christian thinkers. Among the numerous books published through this venture were *Cultural Foundations of Indian Democracy, Problems of Indian*

Democracy, and *Christian Participation in Nation-Building*. The last one is the summing up of the entire study. As the main organ and forum for dialogues, CISRS published a quarterly, *Religion and Society*. A quick glance through the themes of the early years reveals the Institute's engagement with various national issues. In the first six volumes (1954-59), we see such themes as "Socialist Pattern of Society," "Fundamental Rights," "Sarvodaya," "Caste in Church and Nation," "Christian Encounter with Other Faiths" and "Christian Participation in Nation-Building."

Between Devanandan and Thomas, Devanandan focused on the religious dimension while Thomas dealt mostly with social and political issues. As Russell Chandran helpfully classified their contributions, Devanandan initiated a "dialogue theology" with the conviction that Indian theology would be characterized by the interpretation of Christian faith in dialogue with other faiths, and Thomas was a theologian of "liberation and humanisation."[79] Thomas understood sin and salvation as the loss and restoration of true humanity and interpreted humanization as salvation. Devanandan sought dialogue with other faiths on faith issues, and Thomas looked for common humanity for the service of the nation and the world in the dialogue with other faiths. Both as a dialogue partner and as a principle of national existence, Thomas made secularism a major component of his theological engagement.

In the following period, Indian Christian theology was dominated by these two major themes: dialogue with adherents of other faiths and liberative service to human needs. The two theologians picked up the indigenization theology from their predecessors, developed nation-building theology in the critical years of Indian nation-building, and handed over two major theological approaches to their successor-theologians of India: dialogue and liberation. Numerous theologians of different confessional traditions have taken up these theological methods. Thinkers and theologians such as Raymond Pannikar, Stanley J. Samartha, K. P. Aleaze and others have furthered the theology of religions much more, to the extent that Devanandan might not have agreed with them. Thomas' approach of social-political engagement in developing theology has generated liberative approaches for Dalit theology, Indian feminist-womanist theology, and some forms of tribal theology in India. Thus, Indian Christian theology flows out of the Christian dialogical witness among people of other faiths and the Christian social witness to the national and global communities.

If one is to chronicle the development of theological themes in the subsequent period, theological consideration of other religions as a theme as well as partners in theological dialogue came to dominate Indian theological scenes from the 1970s. If theology as absorbed by Hindu philosophy and religious concerns centring around Indian nationality defined Indian theology, such a theology came to be challenged with the Christian theological affirmation of the marginalized outcaste (out-casted from Hinduism) Dalits and non-caste (non-Hindu) tribal people together with the twice-alienated women. To highlight their marginal and subordinated identity, some have conveniently band them together as "subaltern theologies." Because a detailed discussion of this new theology is beyond the scope of this chapter, a cursory mention will be sufficient for our purpose here. God's identification and affirmation of the poor and neglected exemplified by Jesus Christ as reflected in the gospels is recapitulated in these theologies.

Beginning in the 1980s, Dalit and tribal theologies have been made as another distinctly Indian theology. The construction of Dalit and tribal theologies has been done mostly in a resistant mode—as a resistant to their casteist domination in Indian society. The feminist or womanist theology of the Dalit and tribal Christians also takes a distinctly Indian feature with patriarchy as an added layer to the casteist oppression. For this reason, some describe the experience of Indian Christian women as double oppression. In conversation with liberation theologies elsewhere, the dominant theological approach has been liberation. The dominance of charismatic spirituality among these Dalit and tribal Christians is also calling for a charismatic theological affirmation.

Endnotes

[1] C. F. Andrews, *The Renaissance in India: Its Missionary Aspect* (London: Church Missionary Society, 1912), 167.

[2] G. A. Oddie, "Indian Christians and the National Congress," *Indian Church History Review* 2, 1 (June 1968): 53.

[3] Andrews, *The Renaissance in India*, 166.

[4] Quoted by Oddie, "Indian Christians and the National Congress," 51.

[5] *Young Men of India* XIX, 11 (November 1908): 190, quoted in Oddie, 51.

[6] A. J. Appasamy, *The Christian Task in Independent India* (London: SPCK, 1951), 2.

[7] Ibid.

[8] E. C. Bhatty, "The Indian Christian Community and the Nationalist Movement," *NCCR* LXII, 11 (November 1942): 449.

[9] John C. B. Webster, *The Dalit Christians: A History*, Revised and Enlarged (Delhi: ISPCK, 2009), 96-98.

[10] Baj Ranjan Mani, *Debrahmanising History: Dominance and Resistance in Indian Society* (New Delhi: Manohar Publishers and Distributors, 2005), 346.

[11] Ibid.

[12] Webster, *The Dalit Christians*, 114.

[13] Eleanor Zelliot, "Congress and the Untouchables, 1917-1950," in *Nationalist Movement in India: A Reader*, ed., Sekhar Bandyopadhyay, pp. 219-235 (New Delhi: Oxford University Press, 2009), 227.

[14] D. V. Singh, "Nationalism and the Search for Identity in the 19th Century Protestant Christianity in India," *Indian Church History Review* 24, 2 (December 1980): 105-116.

[15] Singh, 113.

[16] The full name of the association was "The Bengal Christian Association for the Promotion of Christian Truth and Godliness, and the Protection of the Rights of Indian Christians." Kaj Baago, "The First Independent Movement among Indian Christians," *Indian Church History Review* 1, 1 (June 1967): 66.

[17] Ibid., 65.

[18] Kaj Baago, *Pioneers of Indigenous Christianity* (Bangalore: The Christian Institute for the Study of Religion and Society; Madras: The Christian Literature Society, 1969), 1-11.

[19] Singh, 107.

[20] Kaj Baago, "The First Independent Movement among Indian Christians," *Indian Church History Review* 1 (1967): 66.

[21] Ibid., 67.

[22] Ibid., 70.

[23] Ibid., 76-77.

[24] George Thomas, *Christian Indians and Indian Nationalism, 1885-1950: An Interpretation in Historical and Theological Perspectives* (Frankfurt am Main et al.: Verlag Peter D. Lang, 1979).

[25] Ibid., 246-252.

[26] M. M. Thomas, *Ideological Quest within Christian Commitment, 1939-1954* (Madras: Christian Literature Society, 1983), 133-148, 236-268. Also see M. M. Thomas, "Indian Nationalism: A Christian Interpretation," *Religion and Society* 6, 2 (June 1959): 4-26.

[27] Ibid, 133-148; M. M. Thomas, "Indian Nationalism: A Christian Interpretation," *Religion and Society* 6, 2 (June 1959): 4-26, especially 11.

[28] Timothy C. Tennent, *Building Christianity on Indian Foundation: The Legacy of Brahmabândhav Upâdhyây* (Delhi: ISPCK, 2000), 7.

[29] Robin Boyd, *An Introduction to Indian Christian Theology*, Revised (Madras: The Christian Literature Society, 1975), 66.

[30] See T. K. Thomas, *The Witness of S. K. George* (Madras: The Christian Literature Society, 1970).

[31] Robin Boyd, *An Introduction to Indian Christian Theology*, revised (Madras: The Christian Literature Society, 1975), 166.

[32] M. M. Thomas, "Toward an Indigenous Christian Theology," in *Asian Voices in Christian Theology*, ed. Gerald H. Anderson (Maryknoll, NY: Orbis Books, 1976), 25.

[33] Susan Visvanathan, "S. K. Rudra, C. F. Andrews, and M. K. Gandhi: Friendship, Dialogue and Interiority in the Question of Indian Nationalism," *Economic and Political Weekly* 37, No. 34 (August 24-30, 2002): 3533.

[34] Ibid.

[35] Quoted from an article in *Young India* in 1925 by Susan Visvanathan, ibid.

[36] A. W. Davies, "Foreign Missions and the Indian Church: The Report of an Informal Conference," *The Harvest Field* 39, 10 (October 1919): 387.

[37] Ibid.

[38] Ibid., 388.

[39] John C. B. Webster, *A Social History of Christianity: North-west India since 1800* (New Delhi: Oxford University Press, 2007), 243.

[40] Ibid.

[41] Ibid., 244.

[42] Two of the founding members were from Burma, one American, and the rest from various parts of today's India, Pakistan, and Sri Lanka. A brief description of each is to be found in *The Founders of the National Missionary Society of India*, compiled by C. E. Abraham (Madras: The National Missionary Society of India, 1947).

[43] Donald Fossett Ebright, "The National Missionary Society of India, 1905-1942: An Expression of the movement toward Indigenization within the Indian Christian Community," A dissertation submitted to the faculty of the division of the Divinity School in the Candidacy for the degree of Doctor of Philosophy, June 1944, The University of Chicago, 236-241.

[44] Quoted by Susan Billington Harper, *In the Shadow of the Mahatma: Bishop Azariah and the Travails of Christianity in British India* (Grand Rapids, MI and Cambridge, UK: Eerdmans, 2000), 297.

[45] V. S Azariah, *India and the Christian Movement* (Madras, Allahabad, Colombo: The Christian Literature Society for India, 1936), 105.

[46] K. T. Paul, *The British Connection with India* (London: Student Christian Movement, 1927), 143.

[47] Ibid., 145.

[48] Ibid., 7.

[49] H. A Popley, *K. T. Paul: Christian Leader* (Calcutta: YMCA Publishing House, 1938), 180.

[50] K. T. Paul, "Indian Christians and the National Movement," *YMI* (January 1909): 3-4.

[51] Kanakarayan Paul, "How Missions Denationalize Indians," *International Review of Missions* 8 (1919): 510.

[52] Ibid., 514.

[53] Quoted in Popley, 194-195.

⁵⁴ "The Present Situation in India: A Message and an Appeal to our Christian Brethren in India and Britain," *NCCR* 50, 7 (July 1930): 342-343.

⁵⁵ See Ainslie Embree, *The Hindu Tradition* (New York: Modern Library, 1966).

⁵⁶ John C. B. Webster, *A Social History of Christianity: North-west India since 1800* (New Delhi: Oxford University Press, 2007), 245.

⁵⁷ D. G. Moses, "Indigenisation," in *Renewal for Mission*, eds. David Lyon and Albert Manuel, Second and enlarged ed. (Madras: The Christian Literature Society, 1968), 75. The first edition was published 1967.

⁵⁸ S. Immanuel David, "The Development of the Concept of Indigenisation among Protestant Christians in India from the time of Henry Venn," *Indian Church History Review* XI, 2 (August 1977): 100-113.

⁵⁹ See Kaj Baago, *Pioneers of Indigenous Christianity* (Bangalore and Madras: The Christian Institute for the Study of Religion and Society, and The Christian Literature Society, 1969), 12; K. P. Aleaz, *Theology of Religions: Birmingham Papers and Other Essays* (Calcutta: Moumita Publishers, 1998), 269-291.

⁶⁰ Baago, *A History of the National Christian Council of India*, 33.

⁶¹ Gurukul Theological Research Group, *A Christian Theological Approach to Hinduism* (Madras: Christian Literature Society, 1956), 4.

⁶² G. V. Job, et al., *Rethinking Christianity in India* (Madras: A. N. Sundarisanam, n.d. [1938]).

⁶³ Vengal Chakkarai Rajasekaran, "The Rethinking Group of Madras: The Champion of Inter-religious Co-operation," *Indian Church History Review* XXVII, 2 (December 1993): 98.

⁶⁴ D. M. Devasahayam and A. N. Sudarisanam, "Preface," *Rethinking Christianity in India*, iii.

⁶⁵ U. Meyer, "Indigenisation – A Critical review of the Discussion in India, 1942-65," *Indian Church History Review* VII, 2 (December 1973): 93.

⁶⁶ See Eddy Asirvatham, "The Christian Message in Relation to the Indian National Situation," in *Rethinking Christianity in India* (Madras: A. N. Sudarisanam, 1938), 227-243.

⁶⁷ Gurukul Theological Research Group, 30.

⁶⁸ Ibid., 50-51.

⁶⁹ F. P. D. Penning, "Publisher's Note," *A Christian Theological Approach to Hinduism* by Gurukul Theological Research Group, v-vi.

⁷⁰ Marcus Ward, *Our Theological Task* (Madras: Christian Literature Society for India, 1946), 1.

⁷¹ Ibid., 3.

[72] Ibid.

[73] Helen Ralston, *Christian Ashrams: A New Religious Movement in Contemporary India* (Lewiston, NY, and Queenston, Ontario: Edwin Mellen, 1987), 26.

[74] S. Jesudason, "The Ashram Method of Training Theological Students," *NCC Review* 62, 7 (July, 1942): 275-283.

[75] R. W. Taylor, "Christian Ashram as a Style of Mission in India," in *Acknowledging the Lordship of Christ: Selected Writings of Richard W. Taylor* (Delhi: ISPCK, 1992): 52-67.

[76] Ralston, 28.

[77] M. M. Thomas, "Indigenization and the Renaissance of Traditional Cultures: A Comment on Vern Rossman's Article," *International Review of Missions* 52 (1963): 191.

[78] P. D. Devanandan, Korula Jacob, and M. M. Thomas, "Preface," *Christian Participation in Nation-Building: The Summing Up of a Corporate Study on Rapid Social Change* (Nagpur: The National Christian Council of India; Bangalore: The Christian Institute for the Study of Religion and Society, 1960), vi-vii.

[79] J. R. Chandran, "Directions of Christian Theology in India," in *For the Sake of the Gospel: Essays in Honour of Samuel Amirtham*, ed. Gnana Robinson (Madurai: TTS Publications, 1980), 23-28.

CHAPTER 3

From a Foreigners' Endeavour to an Indigenous Movement

The Christian Missionary Enterprise in India

In the annals of European Christians missions of the modern era, India occupied a special place. Among the first Jesuit missionaries of the Catholic Church in India was Francis Xavier, a founding member of the Society of Jesus, who began his work in western India in 1542. The first organized mission of the Protestant Church in Europe, popularly called the Danish-Halle mission, sent its first missionaries, Bartholomew Ziegenbalg and Henry Plütschau, to Southern India in 1706. William Carey, often called the "father of modern missions" for initiating a movement of voluntary missionary societies, came to India in 1793 never to leave Indian soil again. Romanticized as a model missionary destination and made the most popular mission field, India probably received more missionaries than any other country during the modern missionary era. The tide, however, turned after India became an independent nation in 1947. What follows is the story of the Christian missionary enterprise in India after independence.

Foreign Missionaries in Independent India

The purpose, continuation, and role of Christian foreign missionaries seem to have occupied the ecumenical Church of India in the 1960s. The National Christian Council of India (NCCI) conducted at least three major consultations on issues surrounding the missionary occupation and identity between 1961 and 1967. The first of these series of consultations, "A Consultation on the Role of Missionaries in India Today" held at Nagpur from October 24 to 27, 1961, asked such questions as "Is he [or she, i.e., the missionary] needed? If needed, for what purpose? What sort of missionary does the Indian Church need now?"[1] Although the questions were quite practical, the papers written from various angles, such as pastoral, educational and medical ministries were theoretical in nature. The second consultation, held in Nasrapur from March 21 to 26, 1966, on "the Mission of the Church in Contemporary India" challenged the Indian church to be missionary and the participants were asked to discern "how God wants His people to be involved, and what he wants them to be concerned about in contemporary India."[2] The third consultation was the most action-oriented in the series. It was held in Nagpur from December 28 to 30, 1967, and dealt specifically with "the missionary issue" and it considered "the presence of missionaries in India in relation to the role of the church."[3] In addition to the delegates from member churches of the NCCI, representatives from the Christian Union of India, the Catholic Union of India and the Association of Indian Christians were present. The consultation was made "necessary," said M. A. Z. Rolston, the Executive Secretary of the NCCI, by "the restrictive measures imposed by the Government of India since September 1966, on the entry and stay of missionaries in India."[4] Eleven days prior to the consultation, leaders and representatives of the NCCI met and consulted the Christian MPs (Members of Parliament) of the Government of India. The MPs gave several "advices" to the churches on issues relating to missionary visas. It is clear that the Indian ecumenical church strongly felt the pressure from the rising nationalistic ethos of the people and the government of India and the challenge brought about by the exiting foreign missionaries.

These consultations clearly signalled a new era of foreign missionary existence in India. Scrutinizing the presentations, discussions, and reports of these consultations, we can deduce the following three crucial challenges encountered by the Indian church then:

(1) the new restrictive measures on missionary visas and the unstable future state of foreign missionary enterprise in India

(2) the anti-missionary attitude in general and anti-conversion feelings in particular of many Hindus, especially the Hindu Communalists

(3) the need for the Indian Church to understand and affirm its missionary call, nature and purpose of existence as a church in the new nation.

Focusing our attention on the missionary enterprise, especially on its historical change and continuance, other important issues, including conversion[5], will not be dealt with here except for their connection with the missionary questions. The report of the consultation in 1967 (the third in the series) includes a report on the Orissa Freedom of Religion bill of 1966, which sought to prevent conversion from one religion to another by force, inducement or any fraudulent means. The report says that Christians fully agree with the bill in condemning conversion by force or fraudulent means, but saw the bill as contravening the freedom to practice and propagate religion as guaranteed by the Constitution of India. In effect, it accused the bill of being unconstitutional. A telegram signed by representatives of the Catholic Union of India, the Christian Union of India, and the National Christian Council was sent to the President of India and the Governor of the state of Orissa asking them to withhold their consent.[6] The bill was clearly understood to be directed against Christians by indirectly accusing them of using inducement and other fraudulent means to convert Hindus, especially of lower caste or outcastes, to Christianity. Rightly or wrongly, the use of inducement had been a popular accusation against missionaries.

The question of foreign missionaries in independent India has a long history. As mentioned before, Christians and missionaries were uncertain about their future during the nationalist movements. In dealing with Gandhi's attitude on conversion, we have mentioned that it was on the question of the future roles of missionaries in independent India that Gandhi made one of his most controversial political statements in 1931. One may argue that the controversial statement, made by the uncontested leader of the nation, set a major precedence for the anti-missionary and anti-Christian sentiment of Hindu communalists in the subsequent period. During the Constituent Assembly meetings between 1947 and 1949, some members of the Assembly expressed their clear misgivings on foreign missionaries. The immediate factor for the change of the policy on missionaries, however, was the reports of large influx of missionaries following the independence of India, especially from independent churches in the USA. As Donald Eugene Smith reported, "The number of Christian missionaries in the country increased considerably after independence, reaching a total of 4683 in 1952.... [R]eports of a large influx of western missionaries were alarming to those who interpreted their presence as a form of continued foreign influence and control."[7] While there was increase in the number of American missionaries, there was also decrease of British missionaries. The National Christian Council of India (NCCI) collected statistics on American missionaries and British missionaries in 1954 which indicated a major decrease (33.75 percent) of the British missionaries from the previous decade (from 1410 in 1937 to 1062 in 1947 and to 934 in 1954) while there was a major increase (roughly 50 percent) of American missionaries in the same period (from 1117 in 1937 to 1675 in 1954).[8]

Beginning in 1952, we see changes in government policies and actions toward foreign missionaries. "About the middle of 1952," reports Korula Jacob of the NCCI, "several missionary societies reported an unprecedented number of refusals of [visa] applications."[9] The National Council inquired with the home ministry of the government of India, and the government's reply was that there was no change of policy. To counter the inaccurate reports of the Government that there was an "enormous increase" of missionaries as well as the ensuing "misgivings," the National Council appealed to the government and asked it to formulate a clear policy.[10] In 1955, the government of India "set forth" a new "procedure" on the admission of missionaries, and the document was widely published in secular newspapers. In communicating the policy in the form of a letter to the National Christian Council of India,[11] the deputy secretary to the Government of India, Fateh Singh, wrote that this was not a new policy but only a new procedure. But since the existence of such a rule was not known before, the new "procedure" was nothing less than a new policy to the Christians. The most significant point of the policy reads, "Those [foreign missionaries] coming for the first time in augmentation … or in replacement [of the existing missionaries] will be admitted into India, if they possess outstanding qualifications or specialized experience" and if Indians are not available for such posts.[12] The most difficult part in dealing with this new policy is the interpretation and application of "outstanding qualifications or specialized experience" to fill positions Indians cannot fill. It also clearly restricted entry of missionaries into border tribal areas of Northeast India by saying "new missionaries coming to work in border and tribal areas ... will not normally be admitted."[13] This new policy had a far-reaching impact on the continuance of foreign missionary enterprise in the following decades leading, as predicted, to "a gradual closure of [foreign] missionary work"[14] in India. The actual strict application of the policy, as seen from the report in the 1967 consultation mentioned above, began in 1966. During the next decade, the number of foreign missionaries sharply declined, and today the missionary visa is extremely difficult to secure.

This restrictive "procedure" concerning missionary visas by independent India cannot but be related to surrounding developments, especially of an anti-missionary nature. In 1954, one year prior to the issuance of the new policy on admission of foreign missionaries, there was a major jolt on the missionary presence in India. This was the formation of the Christian Missionary Activities Inquiry Committee in the state of Madhya Pradesh. The committee, popularly known as "the Niyogi Committee," taking the name of Chairman Bhawani Shankar Niyogi, was set up to inquire into missionary activities in the state. From the beginning, the very selection of the committee and the anti-missionary attitude suspected to be behind the inquiry were resisted and opposed by Christians, especially the Roman Catholic Church. The lone Christian member, a Gandhian nationalist, S. K. George, was considered to be a renegade and was not accepted as qualified to represent Christians.

Just about two years after its formation, the committee submitted its main findings and reported to the state government on April 18, 1956. The report was published in three books of two volumes[15] the same year. The concluding "findings" pointed out the "increase in the American personnel of the Missionary organizations …" and states "Enormous sums of foreign money flow into the country for Missionary work…." "Conversions," it says, "are mostly brought about by undue influence, misrepresentation, etc. or in other words not by conviction but by various inducements offered for proselytization in various forms."[16] In its introductory summary, the report notes, "In all the places visited by the Committee there was unanimity as regards the excellent service rendered by the Missionaries, in the fields of education and medical relief. But on the other hand there was a general complaint from the non-Christian side that the schools and hospitals were being used as means of securing converts."[17]

The committee and its report, "the Niyogi Report" as it came to be called, were seen to be symbolic of the anti-missionary and anti-conversion attitude of Hindu fundamentalists in independent India. The Christians vehemently contested the findings and resisted the recommendations. Although the Report did not have immediate results in the form of new legislation, as Sebastian Kim rightly pointed out, its recommendations became the foundation for the anti-conversion laws under "freedom of religion" acts of the state of Orissa (1967) and Madhya Pradesh itself (1968),[18] and influenced similar laws in other states later. In his study of the impact of the Report, Manohar James concluded that the Report "provided justification for the need to control Christian missionary enterprise and conversions activities in Madhya Pradesh, became a reference guide for Sangh Parivar organizations to systematically stereotype, propagate against and resist Christian conversions in India."[19]

Foreign Missionaries and the Indian Church

Now, as some papers in the consultation suggest, the question is "Does India want foreign missionaries? Do Indian Christians need missionaries? If so, what kind?" The new situation marked a changed condition and ushered in a new period when the number of foreign missionaries would drop significantly and the way Indian Christians would come to assume the missionary witness within India. By and large, creative thinking had been deployed prior to the 1960s, but the new situation forced the Indian church to define itself, and to take responsibility for missionary work within the country. The issue became a part of the Indian Church's effort to indigenize itself to the cultural and national milieu.

Within Christian missionary thinking and discussion, what was called "devolution" of missions had been discussed seriously since the second decade of the twentieth century.[20] Devolution in Christian missions denotes the transfer of power and responsibility from foreign missions to indigenous churches and organizations. Based on the missionary principle, called the "indigenous principle" championed by Henry Venn and Rufus Anderson in the second half of the nineteenth century, the forming of independent indigenous churches which are free from the control of foreign missionaries was placed as an ideal by the principle. In India, as discussed earlier, the national feelings developed among Christians were closely linked to their aspirations for indigenous churches and leadership. As mentioned in the previous chapter, as early as in 1919, the National Missionary Council came to recognize "the growing dissatisfaction ... with [foreign] mission service" among educated Indian Christians, and upon investigation through a conference, found "a growing tension between foreign missions and the Indian Church." It concluded that "the existing breach is ... fundamental," and cannot be healed by "mere improvement in the personal relations between the missionary and the Indian."[21] Despite such early recognition of the problem, significant steps for structural adjustment were not taken for a long time. One missionary is quoted as having said, "It seems strange that to make it [the devolution policy] really effective, it will take the action of a secular government. Still that action would be more welcome, or at least less disturbing, if the motive behind it were as pristine as some of us would like to believe, and if the statement of the religious extremists of other communities seemed less intended 'to smite the shepherd and scatter the sheep.'"[22] New missional thoughts were developed in the form of indigenization and dialogical theologies by Indian thinkers, even as foreign missionaries continued to be the functionaries of the churches. The new policy on missionary visas eventually forced the mission agencies to devolve full responsibility to the Indian churches.

Evangelical Witness and the Explosion of Indigenous Missions

One of the most popular evangelistic efforts in the early years of the twentieth century in India was the movement called "the Evangelistic Forward Movement" which centred in South India, introduced first by Sherwood Eddy and undertaken by the Madras Christian Council from 1915.[23] The movement came to be nationalized through the National Missionary Council. In the 1920s, around the same time as the National Missionary Council was changed into the National Christian Council, according to Kaj Baago, the "evangelistic drive experienced opposition, not from Hindus, but from Christians."[24] Perhaps, the new emphasis on indigenization from this period, as discussed earlier, helped either to broaden the concept of evangelism that challenged the Forward Movement or it questioned evangelism itself. In the Madras Christian Council meeting of 1926, it was decided to drop the name "Evangelistic Forward Movement" stating that it "does not convey today all that the committee is trying to do and also in some cases gives rise to misunderstanding."[25] Baago suggested that social service had replaced evangelism in this period.[26] But from the early 1930s, the "Forward Movement in Evangelism" returned[27] until it was halted by World War II.[28] After the war and the independence of India, in Baago's description, the nationalizing Christianity moved away from evangelism and engaged in serving the social and developmental needs of the nation.

In seeking to Indianize Christianity, the main attention had been focused on indigenization and dialogue with non-Christians. As noble and important as the call for indigenization and dialogical approach were, one may also ask whether the proponents of indigenization and dialogical theologies failed to give equal emphasis to communicating the unique Christ to non-Christian Indians. From all appearances, conscious efforts to intentionally communicate the Gospel to those outside the Christian fold with their Indianized or indigenized message of Christ became increasingly absent. From a missional point of view, the efforts appeared to have neglected the actual communication of the gospel, and thus, were not as meaningful and fruitful as they were intended to be. The Ashram movement seemed to have a great promise, but dwindled both as a Hindu practice and Christian continuance.

Is it the case that an indigenized Christian message in the Brahminic Hindu context would necessarily call for a Christianity that is less organized or unorganized to the extent that an organized effort of evangelism becomes untenable? Identification with the cultural norms and practices does lead to different form of Christian missional witness such as the ashram community living. One must admit the contrasting difference between Christianity and

Hinduism that a very distinct form and meaning of Christianity may be called for in the Hindu context. The possibility and felt-need to develop a distinct form of Christianity in its interaction with Indian cultural and religious practices have been an issue faced at various points in history. Since the time of Roberto de Nobili in the seventeenth century to Keshub Chunder Sen, *Christo Samajes* and the founding of the National Church of Madras (discussed in the previous chapter) in the nineteenth century, the issue has been with us. When, as discussed, the "Rethinking Group" of the early twentieth century raised it in a different form, and since Subba Rao's movement[29] and now the work and movement surrounding Jesu Bhaktas or Christ Bhaktas, the Christian missionary world continues to wrestle with the issue and has not yet settled it with ease.

As the church and the nation transitioned into a new period after the independence and foreign missionaries withdrew in the following decade, there was a major decline in evangelistic ministry, especially among the mainline churches. The decline of the mainline churches' engagement in direct evangelistic witness among non-Christians did not seem to be an accident, but appeared to be largely a response to the pressure felt in the new national context. India as a nation sought a new sense of nationhood among people of different cultures, religions and societies through mutual co-existence. The fear of agitating the national majority and upsetting the frail national unity through what might appear to be self-promoting work of aggressive evangelism might have been an important factor in the decline of evangelistic missions. The ongoing polarization between evangelism and social service in the larger world Christian community may have also helped the trend when the elite leadership took its liberal stance. As M. M. Thomas rightly expressed, the central polarizing question as inherited from the Fundamentalist-Modernist debate was on whether the "essence of the gospel" was on "deliverance of the humans from sinfulness or affirmation of the human vocation to creativity and cooperation with God in creating nature and society according to the purpose of God."[30] Indian Christians came to be divided between those who insisted on evangelistic ministry for rebirth (convert) and those who understood ministry almost exclusively as serving the socio-economic needs of the people. While the latter group seemed to have disdained or reconceived the very term "evangelism," the former understood the mission of the church to be a narrowly defined evangelism. If there were more educated lay persons in the former group, the theologically trained church leadership of mainline denominations dominated the latter. In the understanding of "the mission of the Church," what Thangaswammy said about the "general lines" denoted by "humanity, community, and secularity"[31] represented the position of the theologically trained relatively liberal leadership of the mainline churches. The formation of the Evangelical Fellowship of India in 1951 was largely a protest by the conservative evangelical groups.

Evangelistic Missionary Works by Indigenous Christians

Thus, the practice of mission as direct witnessing evangelistic ministry has been taken up largely by churches on the periphery and by para-church organizations. One can compare the beginning of the modern Protestant missionary movement through the work of William Carey, a self-taught cobbler-pastor of a small dissenting Baptist Church, with the launching of indigenous missionary endeavour in India through small churches and para-church organizations at the margins in the Indian church. This is not, however, to say that mainline Christians are not involved in evangelistic missions. In fact, most of the para-church endeavours are supported and even led by members of the mainline churches. Furthermore, some mainline churches are also deeply involved. Evangelistic resurgence in the Marthoma Church, revival movements in some dioceses of the Church of South India in Tamil Nadu[32] and those in Northeast India contributed in large measure to the rise of the new missionary movement in India. Beginning in the 1950s, there came about some small missionary efforts by Indian Christians which eventually grew into a significant movement by the beginning of the twenty-first century. These new missionary endeavours joined hands with the few older indigenous missionary efforts.

In the history of Indian Christian missionary engagements, the Marthoma Evangelistic Association, established in 1888 to send out missionaries, is the first organized indigenous missionary endeavour. K. Rajendran even claims this association is "the first evangelistic association initiated by Asians."[33] With a humble beginning at a small prayer meeting of 12 Christians, the Association was intended for evangelistic mission among non-Christians from the beginning.[34] Through the leadership of V. S. Azariah, who later became the first Indian Bishop of the Anglican Church, the Indian Missionary Society (IMS) was started in 1903 in Palayamkottai of Tirunelveli district (Tamil Nadu). Two years later, a group of 17 young Indian Christian leaders, again led by Azariah, formed the National Missionary Society on Christmas Day in 1905 at Serampore. As stated in the original constitution under "object" and "membership" of the society, the NMS was established "to evangelize unoccupied fields in India and adjacent countries" as an interdenominational effort. From the beginning, membership has been open to "all Indian Christians" while non-Indians can only become "honorary members."[35] Between the IMS and the NMS, the NMS aimed high and wide, and was well-publicized nationally, but it was the IMS that achieved more on the ground. The IMS grew constantly, even as its founder V. S Azariah himself became its missionary to Dornakal. By 2004, the IMS had 635 missionaries in 20 states.[36] While these new indigenous missions were popularly known with distinctions, other indigenous missionary works were closely related with foreign missions and missionaries. Alongside foreign missionaries, there were native "evangelists" whose works of witnessing through preaching and teaching were not different from, or in many cases better than, the "missionaries" from the beginning of the missions. In many places, these native evangelists were the pioneers in bringing the gospel. There are several significant examples from Northeast India. The first Protestant known to have preached the gospel in today's Northeast India was Krishna Pal of the Serampore Mission who preached among Khasis in 1813; it was through the work of two Garo converts that the first church was established in the Garo district of Meghalaya; an Assamese convert by the name of Godhula was the real pioneer in bringing the gospel among the Ao Nagas.[37] A group of Mizo converts were sent as missionaries by Watkin R. Roberts (who voluntarily accompanied missionaries to Mizoram) in 1910 to southern Manipur with which began the "Thado-Kuki Pioneer Mission."[38]

The rise of indigenous missionary endeavours is difficult to trace also because of the diverse nature of the stories and the complex relations with western missionaries and missions. Beginning in the 1950s, we see new indigenous missionary organizations added to the list. Several denominational missions of indigenous origin and support came into being. To take the Mizo Presbyterian Church as an example, which has been self-propagating from its inception, the missionary works of the church began side by side with the (foreign) missionary works of the Welsh Mission. Not only did it supply the first missionaries of the Thado-Kuki Mission, the Mizo Presbyterian Church had also sent a missionary to the Haflong Hills (North Cachar of Assam) in 1919.[39] Other missionaries (or evangelists) were sent to other ethnic groups within Mizoram from 1925, and in 1953, a separate committee—the Synod Mission Committee—was formed.[40]

In the rise of non-denominational or interdenominational mission works, a major catalyst of the missionary movement was the life and work of the Evangelical Fellowship of India (EFI). The Fellowship's role in the movement was a combination of direct and indirect influence. Two interdenominational and intentionally indigenous new mission organizations are worth mentioning, which came into being in the 1950s and the 1960s. The first one is the Friends' Missionary Prayer Band (FMPB). Started informally from a student prayer group in the Tirunelvelli area of Tamil Nadu in the late 1950s,[41] which was largely a product of the Vocational Bible School movement, the Band grew into a strong and viable mission "movement"[42] and an active mission society. It started sending out missionaries in 1967 to the neighbouring state of Karnataka and from 1971,[43] and began significant works in North India.[44] By the second decade of the twenty-first century, the FMPB had grown to become the largest Indian indigenous mission organization with more than 800 missionaries and more than 700 local evangelists.[45] The second mission, the Indian Evangelical Mission, was formed as the mission wing of the Evangelical Fellowship of India (EFI) in 1965 to reach the un-evangelized areas of India and to challenge Indian churches to mission.[46] Like several other ministerial arms of the EFI, it gradually grew into an independent missionary organization of almost 600 mission staff today.[47]

A strong Indian missionary movement largely directed by denominational and para-church missionary organizations and Pentecostal-Charismatic Churches sprang up in the 1970s and 1980s. Spiritual renewal movements within denominational churches, such as those in the Tirunelvelli Diocese and the South Kerala Diocese of the Church of South India, the Mizoram

Presbyterian and Baptist churches, and the Nagaland Missionary Movement of the Naga Baptist churches, are the major source of the new missionary movement. Not only do these churches carry out active mission works, they bred the spirit of voluntary mission works and in turn produced various para-church organizations. Many of the independent non-denominational or inter-denominational mission organizations are supported by members of these churches. The new movement also revived and strengthened older missionary organizations. For instance, the Indian Missionary Society had only two fields (Dornakal in Andra Pradesh and another in Tamil Nadu) until 1967, when a new field was opened in Orissa and expanded in the 1980s.[48]

Though deficient in several ways, the study done by the Church Growth Association of India on this new missionary movement, published in 1992, provides the first comprehensive picture of the movement.[49] The editor Sam Lazarus described the decade of the 1970s and the 1980s as the period of "mushrooming of Missions,"[50] and the study includes a directory of 103 indigenous mission organizations of India. The growth of Pentecostal-charismatic churches in India during the last three decades of the twentieth century was the result of the active evangelizing works of its missionaries. According to P. T. Abraham of Sharon Pentecostal Fellowship, "In the decade [of] 1970, twenty-one, and in the decade of 1980 another twenty-four more [mission] agencies were started. In 1988 there were 3,661 missionaries working with PCM [Pentecostal-Charismatic Churches] agencies."[51] Closely associated but quite distinct are the indigenous independent churches most of which are charismatic in character. P. Solomon Raj has been researching this group. He found and studied "73 indigenous mission groups in four coastal districts of Andhra Pradesh."[52] Another major factor in the growth of the new missionary movement in India, as rightly pointed out by K. Rajendran, is the non-traditional new "missions with roots in the West", some of which have been significantly indigenized in India. They are: "Union of Evangelical Students of India, Scripture Union, Global Outreach, Youth for Christ, Far East Broadcasting Association, Gospel Recording Association, Operation Mobilisation, India Every Home Crusades, Youth with A Mission, and Every Creature Crusade."[53] These new missions instilled passion and interest in mission in Indian Christians, trained and temporarily employed them, and then supplied Indian missions with effective missionaries.

It is impossible to know how many Indian missionaries are working in India today. But it is clear that there are more "missionaries"[54] in India today than ever before, and almost all of these missionaries are Indians. The impact of this indigenous movement is being felt today especially in places where Christianity had been a small minority, spawning a new Christian movement. Studies such as Wessly Lukose's on the Pentecostal movement in Rajasthan have shown not only tremendous numerical growth, but also the indigeneity of Christianity and the movement.[55] *Christianity Today* did an observational study of the new movement and called it "the world's most vibrant Christward movement."[56] The term "Christward movement" is coined by a leader of Christian movement in North Indian and refers to indigenous inclusive movements to faith in Jesus Christ without necessarily abandoning one's religion. Richard Howell, former General Secretary of Evangelical Fellowship of India, is quoted as having said, "Christward movements are culturally Hindu yet Christian in faith."[57]

The Church Growth Association of India (CGAI) used to trace the growth of missionaries. According to K. Rajendran, there were 543 Indian missionaries in 1972, which grew to 12,000 by

1994.[58] As said earlier, the directory of mission agencies compiled by CGAI in 1992 already contained 103 mission agencies,[59] but a mission prayer book, *Operation World*, already showed 198 such mission agencies in 1993.[60] Although it does not represent the entirety of Indian missionary endeavours, the story of the India Missions Association (IMA) is indicative of the growth of Indian missions. Like a number of other evangelical bodies, it grew out of the initiative of the Evangelical Fellowship of India (EFI). More specifically, it was formed by five mission agencies as a networking agency for mutual cooperation among mission agencies, following the All India Congress on Missions and Evangelism organized by the EFI in March 1977 at Devlali, Maharashtra. It is not a missionary society in itself, but an association or "a national federation of missions" for partnership, sharing of resources, training, and research. By 1990, the membership had grown to 44,[61] and almost doubled to 86 in 1995 with almost 12,000 missionaries.[62] In addition to providing cooperation among the members, its requirement for members for openness and accountability, says Rajendran, "assures credibility"[63] and thus, attracts membership. By the close of the twentieth century in 2000, IMA had 130 member organizations, and by 2018, the membership directory recorded more than 250 members[64] with a total working force of more than 50,000 individuals. As said earlier, the growth of IMA is only indicative of the growth of Indian missionary enterprise, for there are many more agencies outside the association.

Some significant signs of wider mutual cooperation have been emerging among Indian Christians and those involved in missions in India in recent decades. As M. M. Thomas rightly said in 1993, if conservative evangelicals have emphasized deliverance of humans from sinfulness and modernist-liberals the affirmation of the human creativity and cooperation with God, the former have come to "see that Christian atonement and redemption …

take into account the whole person with his/her involvement in society and culture," and the latter "have now come to recognize that all human creativity and creations need deliverance from the spirit of perversity...."[65] This bifurcation of the community-orientations may have to be trifurcated with Pentecostals as the third branch. A certain P. Singh is quoted by the *Christianity Today* study we have mentioned above as saying, "What is the key avenue for communicating the gospel [today]? Evangelicals say, 'Word,' mainliners say, 'Works,' and charismatics say, 'Wonders,' .... All three are legitimate and needed if they point to Christ."[66] In 1994, the National Council of Churches in India and the India Missions Association held a joint consultation on partnership and issued a joint statement on the subject. What was once a major concern of ecumenical theologians, namely a credible witness to the gospel in the form of respectful dialogue with people of other faiths, has become an essential mode of evangelical missions.

Quite close to the teaching of E. Stanley Jones, Stanley Samartha criticized mere "horizontal" conversion and called for a "vertical" conversion.[67] Samartha and Wesley Ariarajah, in promoting interfaith dialogue, called for witness that does not ask people of other religious faiths to leave their religions and cultures to join the church. "The Christian is called not to convert but to witness,"[68] wrote Ariarajah. Commenting on this statement, M. M. Thomas said, "But there is nothing wrong in inviting those who respond positively to the Person of Christ without leaving their religious and cultural community to form fellowships around the Lord's Table and the Word of God as 'part of the Church' within their religious and cultural community-setting...."[69] This is what evangelical Christian leaders in North India today are calling for with their "Christward movements." The new and debated evangelical mission approach called "insider movement"[70] which encourages and cooperates with such movement as the "*Jesu*

Bhaktas" or "*Christ Bhaktas*"[71] can therefore be seen as the practical outworking of what Thomas, Samartha and others have called for.

Endnotes

[1] National Christian Council of India, *A Consultation on the Role of Missionaries in India Today*, Nagpur, October 24 to 27 (n.p, 1966), i.

[2] "Editorial: The Mission of the Church in Contemporary India," *Findings of the National Consultation on the Mission of the Church in Contemporary India* (Mysore: Wesley Press, 1966), 1.

[3] M. A. Z. Rolston, "Preface" to *The Missionary and the Mission of the Church in India: Report of the Consultation on the Missionary Issue held at Nagpur, December 28-30, 1967* (Nagpur: The National Christian Council of India, n.d.), 1.

[4] Ibid.

[5] For further discussion on conversion, see Sebastian C. H. Kim, *In Search of Identity: Debates on Religious Conversion in India* (New Delhi: Oxford University Press, 2003).

[6] *The Missionary and the Mission of the Church in India: Report of the Consultation on the Missionary Issue held at Nagpur, December 28-30, 1967*, 6.

[7] Donald Eugene Smith, *India as a Secular State* (Princeton: Princeton University Press, 1963), 199.

[8] "Number of Missionaries in India," *NCCR* LXXIV, 9 (September 1954): 396-398. The statistics of American missionaries (secured from the State Department in Washington D.C.) includes all missionaries, but the British number excludes Roman Catholics and independent missions.

[9] Korula Jacob, "The Government of India and the Entry of Missionaries," *International Review of Missions* 47 (1958): 411-412.

[10] "Editorials: The Council and the Government," *NCCR* LXXIV, 12 (December 1954): 519.

[11] See the letter "No. 6/28/ 52-F I, Government of India, Ministry of Home Affairs," dated 31 May 1955, in *Revolution in Mission – A Study Guide on the Subject: "The Role of Missions in Present Day India," A Symposium Intended for Further Study and Discussion*, ed. Blaise Levai (Vellore: The Popular Press, 1957), 280-81.

[12] Ibid, 280. See "Editorials: The Government and Foreign Missionaries," *NCCR* LXXV, 5 (May, 1955): 194 for further comments.

[13] "No. 6/28/ 52-F I, Government of India, Ministry of Home Affairs," in *Revolution in Mission*, 280.

[14] K. Jacob, 414.

[15] Volume I contains the historical background of the subject-matter, the findings and the recommendations; volume II (Part A) has the process, including the tours and the questionnaire, and volume II (Part B), the documents gathered, including statements and correspondence. *Report of the Christian Missionary Activities Enquiry Committee, Madhya Pradesh, 1956*, Volume I, Volume II Part A, Volume II Part B (Nagpur: Government Printing Press, 1956).

[16] *Report of the Christian Missionary Activities Enquiry Committee, Madhya Pradesh, 1956*, Volume I (Nagpur: Government Printing Press, 1956), 131.

[17] Ibid., 3.

[18] Ibid., 73.

[19] B. Manohar James, "The Influence of the Niyogi Committee Report of Madhya Pradesh on Hindu Nationalism and Its Resistance to Christian Missions in Independent India," Ph.D. dissertation, Asbury Theological Seminary, Wilmore, KY, 2016, 303.

[20] Daniel J. Fleming, *Devolutions in Mission Administration as Exemplified by the Legislative History of Five American Missionary Societies in India* (New York; Fleming H. Revell Co., 1916).

[21] A. W. Davies, "Foreign Missions and the Indian Church: The Report of an Informal Conference," *The Harvest Field* 39, 10 (October, 1919): 388.

[22] Quoted by Donald Eugene Smith in *India as a Secular State*, 200-201.

[23] K. Baago, *A History of the National Christian Council of India, 1914-1964*, 20-21.

[24] Ibid., 43.

[25] *Bulletin of the Madras Representative Christian Council*, 1926, 12, quoted in Baago, Ibid., 43.

[26] Baago, 43.

[27] Ibid., 50ff.

[28] Ibid., 59.

[29] See Kaj Baago, *The Movement around Subba Rao: A Study of the Hindu-Christian movement around K. Subba Rao in Andhra Pradesh* (Bangalore:, Christian Institute for the Study of Religion and Society, and Christian Literature Society, 1968); and H. L. Richard, ***Exploring the depths of the mystery of Christ : K. Subba Rao's eclectic praxis of Hindu discipleship to Jesus*** (Bangalore: Centre for Contemporary Christianity, 2005).

[30] M. M. Thomas, *The Church's Mission and Post-Modern Humanism: A Collection of Essays and Talks, 1992-1996* (Tiruvalla: Christava Sahitya Samithi; Delhi: ISPCK, 1996), 117.

[31] D. A. Thangasamy, "The Renewal of the Church for its Mission," in *Renewal for Mission*, eds. David Lyon and Albert Manuel (Madras: The Christian Literature Society, 1968), 9-12.

[32] C. Barnabas, "Dynamic Expansion of the Missionary Movements in India," in *Biblical Theology and Missiological Education in Asia: Essays in Honour of Rev. Dr. Brian Wintle*, eds. Siga Arles, Ashish Chrispal and Paul Mohan Raj (Bangalore: Asia Theological Association, Theological Book Trust, Centre for Contemporary Christianity, 2005), 269.

[33] K. Rajendran, *Which Way forward Indian Missions?: A Critique of Twenty-Five Years, 1971-1997* (Bangalore: SAIACS Press, 1998), 55.

[34] Alexander Mar Thoma Metropolitan, *The Marthoma Church: Heritage and Mission*, fifth impression (Tiruvalla: Christava Sahitya Samithy, 2010), 66.

[35] "Appendix I: The Minutes of the |General Meeting held at the College, Serampore, on the Twenty-fifth Day of December 1905," in *The Founders of the National Missionary Society of India*, compiled by C. E. Abraham (Madras: The National Missionary Society of India, 1947), 28.

[36] M. G. Manickam, "Indian Missionary Society, Tirunelveli," in *Emerging Mission: Reporting on a Consultation, Bangalore, India—November 2004*, eds. Mark Oxbrow and Emma Garrow (London: CMS; Bangalore: IEM; Delhi: ISPCK, 2005), 19.

[37] For a detailed discussion of the contributions of native Christians in the evangelization of Northeast India, see Lalsangkima Pachuau, "'Assistants' or 'Leaders'? The Contributions of Early Christian Converts in North-East India," in *Christianity in Indian History: Issues of Culture, Power and Knowledge*, Edited by Pius Malekandathil, Joy L. K. Pachuau, and Tanika Sarkar (Delhi: Ratna Sagar, 2016), 102-118.

[38] The mission was renamed "North-East India General Mission" in 1922. As it expanded and missionaries sent to Burma, the name was changed again to "Indo-Burma Pioneer Mission" sometime in 1925. Vanlalchhuanawma, *Mission and Tribal Identity: A Historical Analysis of the Mizo Synod Mission Board [of the Presbyterian Church of Mizoram] from a Tribal Perspective, 1953-1981* (Delhi: ISPCK, 2010), 128-129.

[39] Ibid., 132-133.

[40] By 2004, the Synod Mission Board of the Mizoram Presbyterian Church had 606 missionaries and 397 evangelists (local) spreading over 334 mission

centres. See Zosangliana Colney, "Mizoram Presbyterian Church Synod Mission Department," in *Emerging Mission,* eds. Oxbrow and Garrow, 26.

[41] C. Barnabas, 270-271.

[42] Samuel T. Kamaleson, "The Friends' Missionary Prayer Band," in *Reading in Third World Missions: A Collection of Essential Documents,* ed. Marlin L. Nelson (Pasadena, CA: William Carey Library, 1976), 128.

[43] http://fmpb.co.in/background.php (accessed January 22, 2011).

[44] http://fmpb.co.in/second_milestone.php (accessed January 22, 2011).

[45] Jason Dharmaraj (Bishop), "100 Years of Cross-cultural Mission and Issues for Today," in *Emerging Mission,* eds. Oxbrow and Garrow, 13 (and footnote 2).

[46] Theodore Williams, "The Indian Evangelical Mission," in *Reading in Third World Missions: A Collection of Essential Documents,* ed. Marlin L. Nelson (Pasadena, CA: William Carey Library, 1976), 132.

[47] http://www.iemoutreach.org/ (accessed January 22, 2011).

[48] http://www.imschennai.com/fields.html (last accessed January 23, 2011).

[49] Sam Lazarus, ed., *Proclaiming Christ: A Handbook of Indigenous Missions in India* (Madras: Church Growth Association of India, 1992).

[50] Lazarus, Preface to *Proclaiming Christ,* iii.

[51] P. T. Abraham, "Pentecostal-Charismatic Outreach," in *Proclaiming Christ,* ed. Sam Lazarus, 101.

[52] P. Solomon Raj, *The New Wine-Skins: The Story of the Indigenous Missions in Coastal Andhra Pradesh, India* (Delhi: ISPCK; Chennai: Mylapore Institute of Indigenous Studies, 2003), xx.

[53] K. Rajendran, *Which Way Forward Indian Missions?: A Critique of Twenty-five Years, 1972-1977* (Bangalore: SAIACS Press, 1998), 56.

[54] The term is used here to include all those involving in the intentional witness to the gospel among non-Christians.

[55] Wessly Lukose, *Contextual Missiology of the Spirit: Pentecostalism in Rajasthan, India* (Oxford: Regnum Books International, 2013). The book was originally written and submitted as a Ph.D. dissertation at the University of Birmingham.

[56] Jeremy Weber, "Incredible Indian Christianity: A Special Report on the World's most vibrant Christward Movement," *Christianity Today* 60, No. 9 (November 2016): 38-47.

[57] Ibid., 46.

[58] Rajendran, *Which Way Forward Indian Missions?* 13, 48. Rajendran quotes S. Vasantharaj Albert, *A Portrait of India III* (Madras: Church Growth Association of India, 1995), 36.

[59] See the directory in Lazarus, ed., *Proclaiming Christ,* 121-147.

[60] Patrick Johnstone, *Operation World* (Carlisle: OM Books, 1993), 276.

[61] Courtesy Mr. Zohmingthanga, Executive Secretary of IMA, North India region, through electronic interview mail, dated January 13, 2011.

[62] Rajendran, 63.

[63] Ibid., 84.

[64] https://www.imaindia.org/gallery/ima%20directroy.pdf. (Last accessed July 30, 2018).

[65] Thomas, *The Church's Mission and Post-modernism,* 117.

[66] Weber, "Incredible Indian Christianity," 44.

[67] Stanley J. Samartha, *One Christ—Many Religions: Toward a Revised Christology* (Bangalore: SATHRI, 1991), 149-150.

[68] Quoted by Thomas, 120.

[69] Ibid., 120-121.

[70] For studies and the debates on the movement, see the various issues of the *International Journal of Frontier Missions* (http://IJFM.org) such as Volume 21: 4 (Winter 2004), Volume 24:4 (Winter 2007), and Volume 26:4 (Winter 2009).

[71] See Jonas Jørgensen, *Jesus Imandars and Christ Bhaktas: Two Case Studies of Interreligious Hermeneutics and Identity in Global Christianity* (Frankfurt am Main, Oxford: Lang, 2008).

PART 2

India's Theologies
in their Religious Contexts

CHAPTER 4

Hindu Reading
of the Christian Scripture
An Indian Theological Hermeneutics

In attempting to articulate a distinct way of reading the Bible in the Hindu- dominated context of India, an Indian Bible scholar, George M. Soares-Prabhu, delineates two prevailing ways of reading the Bible. He calls them "religious reading" and "social reading."[1] Whereas the former pursues "a dialogue with the traditional Indian religiosity," the second (social reading) reads the Bible "in the light of a liberating praxis among the socially oppressed." The rise of Dalit liberation theology[2] in India since the 1980s has elevated and popularized the social reading method almost to the detriment of religious reading. But Christian theologians associated with the Hindu community of India as well as Hindu scholars studying the Bible have been applying the religious reading method. This chapter is on the "religious reading" of the Bible as it applies to the Hindu community. Analysing the way Hindus and Christians of Hindu background received and interpreted the Bible in India, we try to understand how the Bible is communicated to the Hindus in Christian missionary practice.

We may cluster the positive responses of Hindus to the Christian message up to the present under three broad groups. First, there are baptized converts who accepted Christianity with sincere commitment, even to the point of being ostracized by their families and communities. Secondly, there is a growing group who accept the sole lordship of Jesus Christ without being socially converted to Christianity. This group has now been called *Christ-bhaktas* (or "Hindu devotees of Christ").[3] Thirdly, there are those who responded to the teaching of Jesus Christ and the Bible positively but selectively as Hindus and from Hindu viewpoints. To delineate how the Christian teaching of the Bible is most commonly received and understood by Hindus who responded to the Bible and its teaching, we trace their encounter with the Bible in history, together with the accompanying scriptural concepts in Hinduism.

Anyone who has made a comparative study of Hinduism and Christianity would not miss the striking differences between the two religions. From their basic presuppositions about existence to the general worldviews they hold, Hinduism and Christianity operate on different planes. Keith Ward pointed out what is different about the Hindu traditions when he compared Hinduism with the Semitic religious traditions in which "prophets possessed by the Word of God" serve as intermediaries between human beings and the personal, morally just and merciful God. About Hinduism he writes

> There were no prophets who felt challenged by a morally judging God and who issued condemnations on oppressive social systems. There was no development of belief in a historical purpose or goal. And there was little sense of one creator God who stood apart from creation, as a being quite different in kind....[4]

For Christians, the Bible presupposes a linear development of the universe and tells the story of how the entire creation came into being; it then explains how God has been dealing with human beings in history. Hinduism, on the other hand, views the existence of the universe to be without a beginning and presupposes cycles of creation going back through infinite time. Although Hinduism has been thought of mostly in the religious category, since it does not hold a strict sacred-profane separation or a religious-secular dichotomy and because it holds no unifying and universal religious creed, it can be more fittingly described as a system of living, or a civilization.

Given these significant differences, how do we meaningfully communicate Christian beliefs to our Hindu brothers and sisters? This brief study intends to analyse the meaningful communicability of the scriptural message between Hinduism and Christianity by looking into their understandings of their scriptures. The intention is missional in that it seeks to help Christian communicators to bring the biblical message home to their Hindu friends. Meaningful communication of this kind can happen only when one understands the basic Hindu teachings and their concept of scriptures. Our focus is thus on Hindu scriptural interpretation and the Hindu "reception" of Christ and Christianity, from which we try to glean meaningful implications for Christians.

Although the intention is to chart ways of communicating their basic messages meaningfully between the two religions, such a study can be done only within the larger context of the "meeting" between the two religions. As some studies on the history of this encounter have clarified, frank and honest dialogue has been hard to achieve. On the other hand, it seems plausible to argue that the first serious Christian theological encounter with other religions in modern times happened with the Hindus in India. As we will see, the relativistic nature of Hinduism provides room for Hindus to consider seriously the message of Christians from their own

Hindu viewpoint. Thus, the modern theology of religions may be claimed to have begun with the Hindu encounter with Christ and Christianity in India.

Scriptures and their Interpretations in Hinduism

"No other living tradition can claim scriptures as numerous or as ancient as Hinduism; none of them can boast unbroken tradition as faithfully preserved as the Hindu tradition,"[5] wrote Klaus Klostermaier. How do Hindus conceive of their own scriptures, and how does that understanding compare to that of Christians? Hindus classify their scriptures (or sacred authoritative literature) into two main categories: *śruti* ("that which has been heard" or "seen") and *smṛti* ("that which has been remembered"). Because of the human agency in the second and the completeness of divine work in the first, *śruti* is considered more authoritative, while the open-ended *smṛti* occupies a secondary position. This, however, is not to ignore the popularity and efficacy of *smṛti*. As Howard Coward has rightly observed, "It is the *smṛti* scriptures that in practice evoke spiritual experience for the vast majority of Hindus."[6]

Śruti ("that which is heard") is considered "identical with the Veda (literally "knowledge")."[7] The Veda is composed of four collections or books (*Ṛg, Sāma, Yajur* and *Atharva*). Each of these collections has four parts (*Samhitas, Brahmanas, Aranyakas,* and *Upanishads*). These sectional parts are also considered to be chronological in order. "Modern scholars ... consider the *Sahita* section of *Rig* Veda, dated 1200 B.C.E. or earlier, to be the oldest, and the *Upanishads*, dated 500 B.C.E. or earlier, to be the latest."[8] As that which was "heard" or "seen" by ancient sages, the Veda is given highest authority as "revelation" from God. As the revealed word of God, the Vedas are "*apuaruseya*, without human origin," and thus, "free from human fallibility and limitation."[9]

Yet in comparison to the concept of scripture in other religions, the Hindus do not understand the Vedas dogmatically. "The four Vedas are neither sacred history nor doctrine; they are the instruments for the performance of *yajna*, the sacrifice, which stood at the centre of Vedic religion."[10]

Smṛti, often called "tradition," is secondary in authority. It is the sacred literature that connects the heart of the Hindu system with ordinary people in their daily lives. The term is sometimes used in a narrower sense, having an exclusive reference to the scarce authoritative literature, or alternately in a broader and more inclusive sense. This variety in classification also extends to the authority given to the collections, as the authority attributed to the different collections differs widely. In fact, there is no agreement on where *smṛti* ends as it fades into vernaculars and ethno-regional literature. It is open-ended and new writings are assuming their place in it. A good example is "the *Gitanjali* of Rabindranath Tagore (1861-1914)," which, says Anantanand Rambachan, "has already taken its place among India's devotional works'.[11] In its narrow sense, *smṛti* is often used as a reference to the codes of law (*dharmasastras*). Within this collection, some such as *Manu-Smṛti, Yajnavalkya-Smṛti,* and *Visnu-Smṛti* "rank very high"[12] in the authoritative literature. *Itihāsa* (history), which comprises the two ancient epics, the *Mahabharata* and *Ramayana*, and the *Purānas* (ancient books) are the other authoritative collections within *smṛti*. As the Vedic religion began to fade and the new devotional (*bhakti*) movement became popular, some parts of *smṛti*, such as the *Bhagavad Gita* of the *Mahabharata* gained significant authority and popularity. The *Gita*, as it is known, became such a popular scripture that many leaders, including Mahatma Gandhi, took it as a governing text for their lives.

How do Hindus use and interpret their scriptures? What role do the scriptures play in the lives of the many millions of Hindus? Before we deal with the more formal, better-defined, and authoritative *śruti*, we may briefly highlight the role and use of *smṛti*. Although secondary in its authority, it is the *smṛti* collection that directly feeds the spiritual and social life of the vast majority of Hindus in their day-to-day lives. Harold Coward has rightly observed, "The epics, *puranas,* and *tantras*...became the basis for widespread popular devotion in the many regional languages of India...." Furthermore, "Since the Hindu religion has no institutional or church basis," he adds, "these texts are the heart of Hindu life."[13] On the importance of *Itihāsa* and *Purāna* in the intellectual and religious thoughts of Hindus, Klostermaier said,

> Itihāsa-Purāna is in a very real sense the heart of Hinduism, with all its strength and weaknesses...They have shaped Hindu religious and theological terminology and have become the medium for imparting secular knowledge as well. They are the source of much of Indian sociology, politics, medicine, astrology, and geography. Reading Itihāsa-Purāna one can recognize the character of the Indian people, enlarged, typified and idealized - true in an uncanny sense.[14]

In the Hindu socio-religious hierarchy or caste system, the priestly Brahmins are at the top. They are the only people endowed with the privilege of studying the Vedas. It is their duty to study, recite, and teach the Vedas. Since the Vedas are learned, recited, and transmitted orally, the technique of doing that, called the six *Vedangas*, is very important. They are considered "limbs of the Vedas."[15] The six *Vedangas* are phonetics for correct intonation (*Siksha*) of the verses (*mantras*), grammar, meter, etymology, proper timing of rituals, and the process of the rituals themselves. In the learning of the Vedas, intonation and correct use of phrases are important, as are the understandings of the meanings.[16]

The verses from the Vedas are used in sacrifices as well as in other public and private rituals, including life-cycle rites, consecrations of icons and offerings. Daily chanting (*japa*) of scripture verses (*mantra*) is a religious practice for all Hindus, while only the Brahmins have daily *Gayatri Mantra*. The use of scripture in Hindu experience is predominantly oral in nature. To quote Harold Coward, "In the conduct of religious rituals individual devotees chant verses of scripture (mantras) from memory or after the priest...In Hindu spiritual experience the chanting of such mantras puts one in direct touch with the divine power...By concentrating one's mind on such a mantra, through repeated chanting, the devotee invokes the power inherent in the divine intuition and so purifies consciousness."[17] While Hinduism is steeped in rituals, the meanings of Scriptures are equally important. If the Vedic hymns are mostly for rituals, the Upanishads (often called "Vedanta" meaning "end of the Veda") lay out philosophies of life and meanings of existence. The Upanishads are the foundations of Hindu philosophy, and philosophers of different schools comment on them with varying distinctions. These schools are very different and even seemingly contradictory in their philosophies, which is a reflection of Hinduism itself. In Hinduism, different ways and means can coexist without cancelling each other, and thus plurality characterizes the Hindu way of thinking.

The highest religious goal is liberation (*moksha*) from the cycle of rebirth. There is not just one way to reach that goal. There are at least three major paths to this highest goal: the path of knowledge (*jnanamarga*), the pat h of works and purity (*karmamarga*), and the path of devotion (*bhaktimarga*). Truth is many-sided, and the meaning of truth varies according to the different schools of philosophy.

Because of their connection to theologizing in the Hindu context, the sources of knowledge or *pramāṇas* are very important. An Indian Christian religious scholar K. P. Aleaz lists six sources of knowledge recognized by Indian philosophy: perception (*pratyaksha*), inference (*anumāna*), testimony (*shabda*), comparison (*upamāna*), postulation (*arthāpatti*) and non-cognition (*anupalabdhi*).[18] While the Advaita school recognized all six sources, other schools recognized some and excluded others. On one source they all agree, according Rambachan, that is, *shabda* (Scripture or testimony),[19] which testifies to the importance of scripture in the Hindu philosophies. Indian Christian theologians have attempted to adapt these *pramāṇas* in their contextual theological interpretations.[20]

Hindu-Christian Interaction

"Despite its long presence in India, Christianity does not seem to have impinged on Hinduism to any remarkable degree...till after the establishment of the British Raj in India,"[21] commented Arvind Sharma. As part of their attempt to communicate the message of the gospel, missionaries came to learn elements and aspects of the religion. Geoffrey Oddie has shown how missionaries, drawing their knowledge from their Hindu Pundits-informants, encountered difficulties in acquiring any comprehensive knowledge about Hinduism.[22] Their motivation to convert Hindus, alongside some missionaries' lack of respect for the religion, made the missionaries' knowledge of Hinduism susceptible to doubts by Hindus. Interest in understanding Hinduism for its own sake among Westerners in the colonial context began outside the missionary circle in the late eighteenth and early nineteenth centuries. A group of rationalists, including Sir William Jones, H. T. Colebrook, Charles Wilkins and H. H. Wilson, began what came to be called Indological studies by translating a number of Hindu scriptures.[23] In the course of the nineteenth century, they were followed by other scholars, often referred to as "Orientalists," such as Friedrich Max Mueller, who changed the future of the study of Asian religions with the publication of his monumental *Sacred Books of the East*.[24] On the Hindu side, serious and respectful consideration of the Christian gospel began in the 1820s with reformist Ram Mohun Roy.

The Hindu response to Christianity cannot be studied in isolation from its encounter with modernization from the West through colonization. Hindus reacted to the intruding civilization quite slowly. "Up until the beginning of the nineteenth century there is very little indication of the reaction of Indians to the ideas and values of the West, even though there was opportunity at least from the beginning of the fifteenth century for cultural interchange,"[25] wrote Ainslie Embree. Although one should be very careful not to conflate or confuse colonialism with the Christian missionary enterprise, both were heavily influenced by the modernization project of the West. From the native viewpoint, especially before the middle of the nineteenth century, it would be difficult to differentiate colonialism, modernization, westernization, and Christianity. If Hindus understood modernization and westernization as synonyms, they also saw Christianity as a part of the mix. The close connection between religion, culture and society in Hinduism would support such a conflation in the understanding.

As diverse as Hindus were in their philosophies and religious viewpoints, their response to Western modernization was also diverse. Embree identified four responses: (1) "indifference," (2) "acceptance of everything Western" by rejecting "the old tradition," (3) "critical and selective" acceptance to "reform" society, and (4) "outright and hostile rejection of the values and ideas of the Western world."[26] Because of the diversity of responses even within each of these, it may be better to use these four as common markers in a spectrum of responses. These markers help to identify some common responding positions that can be loosely categorized together. For instance, some of the reformers (group 3) did so with a rather hostile response to the West and sought to revive Hinduism by reforming it. They may belong to both the third and fourth categories. Those in the first two categories left little or no impact on the ensuing history of Hindu-Christian interaction. The third and fourth responses redefined Hindu-Christian relations and changed the course of India's history itself. While the new tradition that emerged from the reformist line led India as a nation to become a modern "secular" state, the teachings and influence of the rejectionists later resurfaced in different forms as challenges and impediments to Indian secularism. Because of the seriousness with which they consider the biblical teachings, we focus on the reformists and the tradition that followed.

Hindu Reformation, Revival, and Christianity

Two reforming societies, the Arya Samaj and the Brahmo Samaj represented opposite stances on Christianity and Western society. The Arya Samaj, founded by Dayananda Saraswati, gave absolute authority to the four Vedas and interpreted them as teaching monotheism. Not only did Saraswati strongly oppose Christianity and western values, he was also critical of contemporary polytheistic Hinduism. To quote his words against Christianity and its scriptural teaching:

> The Christians go about preaching 'Come, embrace our religion, get your sins forgiven and he [sic] saved.' All this is untrue, since had Christ possessed the power of having sins remitted, instil faith in others and purifying them, why would he have not freed his disciples from sin, made them faithful and pure [?]…Now disciples of Christ were destitute of as much faith as a grain of

mustard seed and it is they that wrote the Bible, how could then
such a book be held as an authority [?][27]

The Brahma Samaj, on the other hand, seriously considered
modern education and technology for the benefit of Hinduism
and adapted them for Hindu tradition. The founder of the
movement, Rajashri Ram Mohun Roy, initiated serious studies of
Christianity. His and his followers' responses to Christianity paved
the way for indigenous Indian theology. With the publication of
his *The Precept of Christ* in 1820 and the ensuing debate with
Joshua Marshman of Serampore Mission,[28] Roy publicized his
morally-driven monotheism for the reform of Hindu society. As
with most other Hindu intellectuals' reflections on the Bible in
the ensuing period, Roy was fascinated by the great teachings of
Jesus, but would not affirm him as divine or believe in his atoning
sacrifice.[29] Roy's theological position became typical of one Hindu
intellectual response to the Christian faith in the years to come.
His monotheistic religion eventually led him toward Unitarianism.

The progressive tradition that emerged out of this reforming
spirit broadened and eventually helped the renascent Hinduism
of the twentieth century. This emergent Hinduism produced a
new breed of the religion, often called "Neo-Hinduism." In being
open to modernity, especially its educational and technological
aspects, the reformists and the emergent Neo-Hindus facilitated
this openness largely by introducing modernizing changes to
the Hindu tradition. In other words, to facilitate change, they
connected modern ideas with the Hindu tradition. As discussed
earlier, Mahatma Gandhi provided a prime example of the fusion
between modern thinking and Hindu traditions.

While Roy and most other Neo-Hindus who followed him
lacked a religious commitment to the Christian teaching of Christ,
one of Roy's successors in the Brahmo Samaj, Keshub Chandra

Sen, did not. Considered by some to be "the most innovative, charismatic, and influential Hindu religious reformer of the nineteenth century,"[30] Keshub Chandra Sen produced some of the best theological expositions using Hindu religious tradition. Christocentric in his religious faith while self-consciously Hindu, Sen provided an in-depth exposition of kenotic Christology using John's theology of the oneness of God and Christ (Father and Son).[31] He used the *advaitins'* (proponents of non-dualistic understanding of Brahman in the Upanishad) theological description of the Brahman (or the Ultimate Reality) as *Sat, Cit, Ananda* (being, intelligence and bliss) creatively to interpret the meaning of the Christian concept of Trinity. In this as well as in the theology of fulfilment and the hidden Christ of Hinduism, he was to be followed by other Indian Christian theologians.[32] Confessedly eclectic, he was considered by Hindus to be Christian, but Christians considered him a mere eclectic Hindu and a strong critic of the church and missions in India.

The Brahmo Samaj, as a reforming society of Brahmanism, arose as a response to both modernization and Christianity. Consciously or otherwise, its organizational scheme and sense of societal identity seemed to have been adapted from the Christian churches. Given the non-institutional character of Hinduism, this was a radical move. Keshub Sen went further by proposing what he called "the Church of the New Dispensation," which he idealized as the ultimate amalgamation of the best of Christianity and Hinduism. Not only did he fail in promoting the church, but the church never realized any organizational existence. However the attempt points to the possible character of an indigenous church in a Hindu context. The attempt strongly influenced Christians to look for a united indigenous church as discussed earlier.

Most Hindu intellectuals who made meaningful responses to the Christian message learned the teachings from direct contacts with Christians. But there was one significant and influential Hindu "theologian" who responded to Christ positively without any direct and formal interaction with Christians. His name was Sri Ramakrishna. After hearing portions of the Bible read to him by a Hindu friend, Ramakrishna had an extraordinary experience of a divine expression of Christ while gazing at the picture of the child Jesus in his mother's lap.[33] Like many other Hindus, Ramakrishna came to accept Jesus Christ as an incarnation of God. Two things distinguished him from others, however: his experiential methodology and his own feeling of identity with Jesus through his growing consciousness as Jesus' incarnation. Ramakrishna's was a religion of inclusivity, as he sought authentic religious experience in different religious traditions. He became one of the most influential spiritual leaders of India in modern times. If Christians found it difficult to accept his consciousness of being an incarnation, he was critical of the Christians' emphasis on sin and their exclusive truth claims.

If one combines the positions of Ram Mohun Roy and Sri Ramakrishna, one can perceive the main trend of Neo-Hindu views of Christ and Christianity. Yet other Neo-Hindu thinkers are more critical towards Christianity than Roy and Ramakrishna. If some are more combative against Christians than others - people such as Swami Vivekananda, whose vibrant and courageous criticism of Christianity during his trip to North America earned him the nickname of "the cyclonic monk of India"[34] - others such as Gandhi identify closely with Jesus, Gandhi claimed to be more Christian than many so-called Christians[35] while rejecting Jesus as the only son of God, as well as his atoning work.[36] The one common thread is the respect for Jesus Christ given to him without claiming him to be the saviour. The main theological agenda of Hindu intellectuals includes:

1. A deep respect for the moral teachings and examples of Jesus Christ with no faith in the atoning effect of his death for salvation.

2. A strong monotheism accompanied by a firm faith in Jesus as God's incarnation without excluding other incarnations.

3. A respectful but selective reading of the Bible, especially those passages on moral and exemplary teachings.

4. A critique of Christians on moral grounds for their cultural and political domination as well as their exclusive truth claims.

A Christian Reflection and Some Observations

Thus far, we have deliberately focused on the Hindu concept of scripture and the response to the Christian message. As we have discussed above, Keshub Chandra Sen and others who followed him in the later history of Brahmo Samaj went further with their Christocentric affirmations. In fact, a few of those associates influenced by Sen became Christians; among them were Brahmabandhab Upadhyaya and Manilal Parekh. Upadhyaya later described himself as a Hindu-Christian with his distinct Vedist (and later Vedantin) theology. Before we close this brief study with some observations, let me mention how we may outline the development of Christian thought in its interaction with Hindu responses. There are a few writings tracing the development of Hindu-Christian interactions with a wide variety of approaches. For instance, Bob Robinson[37] focuses on process among Indian scholars and leaders, and Wesley Ariarajah[38] locates the subject within the ecumenical history of the World Council of Churches. Overall, the development may be captured under these headings: (1) the various missionary approaches ranging from proselytizing confrontations to life-sharing transformations; (2) the Ashram (community living) approach; (3) pluralistic relativism; (4) roundtable dialogical approach; and (5) being Christian within Hinduism (Hindu devotees of Christ), which some called the "insider movement." Since it is beyond the scope of the present study, we will not deal with these points in this chapter.

We may close by drawing out the implications of this discussion for the current realities of Christian witness among the Hindus. First, we must recognize the profound differences between the two religions. For any meaningful communication between them, the foundational worldview of each needs to be taken into serious consideration while being faithful to the tradition. The tension between openness to other traditions and faithfulness to one's own tradition is true in all religions. While some features of Hinduism are definite and exclusive, other parts are imprecise and inclusive. The *śruti* is clearly defined and its authority unquestioned. But the *smṛti* has no clear boundary and is vested with a great deal of inclusivity. While *smṛti* is secondary in authority, it is primary in its direct influence on the human life. The Hindu intellectuals who responded positively to Christ and the Bible seem to have done so because of the secondary *smṛti* authority and its vague bounded-ness. The Bible can easily be included as a part of *smṛti* or given a place of equivalence. The selectiveness of what is affirmed and what is rejected in the biblical teachings seems to reflect the place of selection in the *smṛti*.

The open-endedness of Hinduism, especially through the *smṛti* channel and the tradition's relativism, make Hinduism open to other spiritual paths as long as these do not exclude others. Much of what we now identify as the theology of religious pluralism not only resonates with the thoughts of Neo-Hindus such as Gandhi and Radhakrishnan, but is actually founded on the teachings of these Neo-Hindus. In other words, the founding inspiration of pluralist theology is what Radhakrishnan calls "the hospitality of the Hindu mind" which accepts almost all varieties of beliefs and doctrines and treats them "as authentic expressions of spiritual endeavours, however antithetic they may appear to be."[39] This relativism of Neo-Hindu teaching has left an indelible mark on Christian theology of religions as it spawned a relativist theology of pluralism.

The strength of Hindu tradition is shown in its powerful hold on the identity of its adherents. For most Hindus who have responded positively to Christ and to biblical teaching, including converts who have affirmed Christ's atoning work and have been baptized, the longing to combine Christian and Hindu Scriptures and to identify with Hindu tradition has been strong. The degrees to which they desire this seem to vary. Brahmabandhav Upadhyaya, who famously called himself "Hindu-Catholic" even as the Catholic Church was distancing itself from him once said, "By birth we are Hindus and shall remain Hindu till death. But as *dvija* (twice born) by virtue of our sacramental rebirth, we are Catholics, we are members of the indefinable communion embracing all ages and claims."[40] Later in his life, the Rev. Yisu Das (1911-1997), a Methodist minister and theological teacher, identified himself as a "Christ *Bhakta*" and said he experienced Jesus Christ as his *ishtadevata*, *saguna* Brahman and *shabda* Brahman, his guru and the image of God.[41] The life story of N. V. Tilak, M. C. Parekh, and even such an evangelical figure as R. C. Das show deep affinity to reading the Bible from the Hindu viewpoints.

In his inquiry of how Hindus would respond to the Christian proclamation of Jesus Christ as the life of the world, an Indian

Catholic thinker, Samuel Ryan, raised an important question of how such a proclamation might be done from within.

> Is it at all possible to bring life or be life to, or share life with, any tradition or situation, secular or religious, while remaining outside it, without becoming enfleshed in it, without giving ourselves to it in firm commitment and deep involvement, without immersing ourselves in the Jordan of its cultural and religious reality and participating in its life, its wealth, its poverty, its limitations, struggles and agony?[42]

Ryan strongly suggested that Christians enter into Hindu tradition and en-flesh life from within. "When we speak a global word about Jesus and present him as the life of the world," he continued, "it is incumbent upon us to help that word become incarnate in global reality. Not only are the world cultures to become its body, but the world religions as well as every .uest and God experience."[43] Inspired by an empirical finding of positive Hindu responses to Christ outside the church[44] as well as other contextual missiological endeavours in world religions, a group of evangelical missiologists advocates an insider effort along similar lines.[45] In this endeavour, one may need to determine if and how the biblical message might be given not only the secondary (*sm ti*) role, but also the *ruti* primacy status. Such an enterprise will need time and consistency. We may draw a lesson from the Hindu concept of time and its stress on time-proven tradition; Christians should refrain from haste and impatient communication in their ministries. There is no room for haste in the Hindu world. The biblical message and essential Christian beliefs will have to be translated into practical and realistic living principles. Just as we began this chapter with the words of George M. Soares-Prabhu, we close with his words again. He wrote, "An Indian exegesis ... [is] greatly concerned about relevance... Relevance has always been the goal of traditional Indian (Hindu) theology, where a study of the sacred books was never merely an academic exercise ("truth for truth's sake") but always a severely practical quest after liberation."[46]

Endnotes

[1] George M. Soares-Prabhu, S.J., 'Towards an Indian Interpretation of the Bible,' in *Biblical Themes for a Contextual Theology Today: Collected Writings of George M. Soares-Prabhu, S.J.* Vol. 1. Ed. Isaac Padinjarekuttu (Pune: Jnana-Deepa Vidyapeeth, 1999), 216.

[2] Both describing and prescribing liberation of the 'outcastes' of Hinduism from their oppressive condition, Dalit theology is an Indian liberation theology. Dalits (often referred to as 'outcastes' or 'untouchables' because of 'impurity') comprise the largest group within the Indian Christian community.

[3] For a study of this movement in South India, see Dasan Jeyaraj, *Followers of Christ Outside the Church in Chennai, India: A Socio-Historical Study of a Non-Church Movement.* Zoetermeer: Boekencentrum Academic, 2010. For a study in North India, see Vinod John, 'Believing without Belonging?: Religious Beliefs and Social Belonging of Hindu Devotees of Christ, A Case Study in Varanasi' (Ph.D. diss., Asbury Theological Seminary, Wilmore, KY, 2013).

[4] Keith Ward, *Religion and Revelation* (Oxford: Clarendon Press, 1994), 135.

[5] Klaus K. Klostermaier, *A Survey of Hinduism*, third ed. (Albany, NY: State University New York Press, 2007), 45.

[6] Harold Coward, 'The Experience of Scripture in Hinduism and Christianity,' in *Hindu-Christian Dialogue: Perspectives and Encounters*, ed. Harold Coward (Maryknoll: Orbis Books, 1989), 233.

[7] Klaus K. Klostermaier, *Hindu Writings: A Short Introduction to the Sources* (Oxford: One World, 2000), 4.

[8] Anantanand Rambachan, "Hinduism," in *Experiencing Scripture in World Religions*, ed. Harold Coward (Maryknoll, NY: Orbis Books, 2000), 89.

[9] Ibid. 91.

[10] Klostermaier, *A Survey of Hinduism*, 47.

[11] Rambachan, 99.

[12] Klostermaier, *Hindu Writings*, 5.

[13] Harold Coward, *Sacred Word and Sacred Text: Scripture in World Religions* (Maryknoll, NY: Orbis Books, 1988), 110-111.

[14] Klostermaier, *A Survey of Hinduism*, 59-60.

[15] Rambachan, 93.

[16] Ibid., 93-94.

[17] Coward, "The Experience of Scripture in Hinduism and Christianity," 235.

[18] K. P. Aleaz, *The Role of Pramâòas in Hindu-Christian Epistemology* (Calcutta: Punthi-Pustak, 1991), 12.

[19] Rambachan, 103.

[20] A. J. Appasamy, *What shall we believe?: A Study of the Christian Pramâòas* (Madras, Delhi, Lucknow: CLS, ISPCK, LPH, 1971); Aleaz, 68-71, 118-119.

[21] Arvind Sharma, preface to *Neo-Hindu Views of Christianity*, ed. Arvind Sharma (Leiden et al. : E. J. Brill, 1988), vii.

[22] Geoffrey A. Oddie, "Hindu Pundits and Missionary 'Knowledge' of Hinduism," in *India and the Indianness of Christianity: Essays on Understanding— Historical, Theological, and Bibliographical—in Honor of Robert Eric Frykenberg*. Ed. Richard Fox Young (Grand Rapids, MI: Eerdmans, 2009), 158-180.

[23] Eric J. Sharpe, *Faith Meets Faith: Some Christian Attitudes to Hinduism in the Nineteenth and Twentieth Centuries* (London: SCM Press, 1977), 10.

[24] Published by Oxford University Press in 50 volumes from 1879 to 1910.

[25] Ainslie Embree, ed. *The Hindu Tradition: Readings in Oriental Thoughts* (New York: Vintage Books, 1972), 275.

[26] Ibid. 275-76.

[27] Ibid., 307.

[28] See the debate between Roy and Joshua Marshman in M. M. Thomas, *Acknowledged Christ of the Indian Renaissance* (London: SCM Press Ltd., 1969), 1-29.

[29] Robin Boyd, *An Introduction to Indian Christian Theology* (Delhi: ISPCK, 1989), 19-26.

[30] David Kopf, "Neo-Hindu Views of Unitarian and Trinitarian Christianity in Nineteenth Century Bengal: The Case of Keshub Chandra Sen," in *Neo-Hindu Views of Christianity*, ed. Arvind Sharma (Leiden et al. : E. J. Brill, 1988), 106.

[31] Boyd, *An Introduction to Indian Christian Theology*, 29.

[32] Ibid., 34-38.

[33] H. W French, "Reverence to Christ Through Mystical Experience and Incarnational Identity: Sri Ramakrishna," in *Neo-Hindu Views of Christianity*, ed. Arvind Sharma (Leiden et al. : E. J. Brill, 1988), 68.

[34] H. W. French, "Swami Vivekananda's Experience and Interpretation of Christianity," in *Neo-Hindu Views of Christianity*, ed. Arvind Sharma (Leiden et al. : E. J. Brill, 1988), 87.

[35] M. K. Gandhi, *Christian Missions: Their Place in India*, ed. Bharatan Kumarappa, second ed. (Ahmedabad: Navajivan Publishing House, 1941, 1957), 33.

[36] M. K. Gandhi, *The Message of Jesus Christ*, ed. Anand T. Hingorani (Bombay: Bharatiya Vidya Bhavan, n.d.), 23.

[37] Bob Robinson, *Christians Meeting Hindus: An Analysis and Theological Critique of the Hindu-Christian Encounter in India* (Oxford: Regnum Books International, 2004).

[38] S. Wesley Ariarajah, *Hindus and Christians: A Century of Protestant Ecumenical Thought* (Grand Rapids, Mich: W.B. Eerdmans Pub. Co, 1991).

[39] S. Radhakrishnan, "Hinduism," in *Cultural History of India*, ed. A. L. Basham (Oxford: Clarendon Press, 1975), 70.

[40] Quoted from Thomas, *Acknowledged Christ of the Indian Renaissance*, 107.

[41] Quoted in Ravi Tiwari, *Reflections and Studies in Religion* (Delhi: ISPCK, 2008), 153.

[42] Samuel Ryan, S.J., "How will the Hindu hear?" *International Review of Mission* 71, No. 281 (January 1982): 54.

[43] Ibid., 55.

[44] See Herbert E. Hoefer, *Churchless Christianity* (Pasadena, CA: William Carey Library, 2001).

[45] For an example of its approach, see H. L. Richard, *Hinduism: A Brief Look at Theology, History, Scriptures, and Social System with Comments on the Gospel in India* (Pasadena, CA: William Carey Library, 2007).

[46] Soares-Prabhu, S.J., 216.

CHAPTER 5

Theology in the Mould of Primal Worldviews

A Case Study of Mizo "Sakhua" in Transition

Introduction

Etymology teaches us that original meaning of a word does not always prevail. What a word originally meant may be lost in the course of its usage. Words accumulate meanings and even result in dislodging their original meanings. One such word, I would argue, is the Mizo word for religion "*sakhua.*" In its original use, *sakhua* has a much narrower meaning in traditional Mizo society than what we now understand religion to be. Because the word has been used to translate (i.e., used as the equivalence of) the English word "religion," all that which conceptually accompanied religion in the English word has been gradually imported as the meaning of *sakhua,* inundating the original meaning. This resulted in a certain confusion as to the content and meaning of traditional Mizo religion (or primal religion). Because of the choice of *sakhua* to "translate" religion, the search for the primal religion of the Mizos has often been done within what *sakhua* refers to in Mizo traditional society.[1] But religion means more than the practice of *sakhua* in traditional society, and the search for Mizo religion should also go beyond traditional *sakhua*. Furthermore, the onslaught of modern western thought with its clear dichotomy between what is sacred and what is secular (under "church and state") has deeply influenced existing descriptions of the primal religions of the tribal people. Such a framework is foreign and its imposition fails to do justice to the integrity of the religious concept.

Studies on Mizo primal religion have suffered acutely from these two methodological flaws and to suggest a way out is a daunting task. Any study on the primal religion of most tribal groups such as the Mizos must avoid the highly western sacred-profane dichotomy and look at the entire socio-cultural life system for the meaning of the people's religion and religiosity even if the term *sakhua* is to be used for religion. This is because of the absence of a clear-cut sacred-profane dichotomy in tribal and in many other eastern people's worldview. The interconnectedness of all aspects of life in the society and the interlocking meanings of symbols of various domains of life do not permit such clear dichotomy, as life is seen and treated as one whole.

The purpose of this chapter is not primarily to re-conceive the nature and content of Mizo primal religion, but to re-examine forms of continuity and change between the primal religion and the Christian religion of the Mizo people today. Focusing primarily on the early message and understanding of Christianity, I will try to highlight some distinctive channels of Christianization among the Mizos and the emergent Mizo Christianity. Do "religions" of the people simply die when the people "convert" to another religion? Without doubting the conversion-event and the tremendous change Christianity has ushered in to the community, I am going to argue that traditional primal religion as well as religiosity live on in some form to become a foundation for the newly embraced Christian religion. In turn, it distinguishes Mizo Christianity and produces some distinctly Mizo theology. I will first look at the traditional religion briefly and try to identify its "rebirth," so to speak, in Mizo-Christian thought. The chapter is intended as an example in the birth of a distinct theology from lived Christianity which is shaped by change and continuity of cultural traditions. Such an experience of change and continuity in the formation of an indigenized theology is not a distinctive Mizo experience. As B. L. Nongbri has shown, such an experience of change and continuity impacting Christian was thinking was deeply felt by the Khasi Christians.[2]

Fundamental Features of Mizo Primal Religion

What is religious and what is not religious in a close-knit society such as Mizo is difficult to determine. What we can try to identify is what fundamentally constitutes the religion in a wide sense of the term. Essentially, the belief in the Supreme Being(s) (or Spirit/s); the belief in the existence and activities of benevolent and malevolent spirits, and the accompanying propitiatory sacrifices to them; the practice of *sakhua*; the belief in life after death and the "religious" striving to reach heaven (*pialral*), constitute the Mizo religion. These beliefs and practices may at first cast an utterly otherworldly image of the religion, but one should note that these beliefs and practices were impelled by the strong communal spirit in the society, and could not be isolated from the everyday affairs of the community. Furthermore, the community festivals and the moral code of behaviour and etiquette in the form of taboos and other superstitious beliefs that regulate and sustain social life of the community serve as resources and form parts of the religion.

So crucial were the communitarian nature and value that one can argue that they prescribe the religious demands to suit the societal needs. This is in line with Emile Durkheim's description of religion as "something eminently social."[3]

God and the Benevolent Spirits

The beliefs and practices that form the core of Mizo religion we have stated above appear to be in a crude state, as they do not seem to be meaningfully connected with one another. It has now generally been agreed that the Mizos believed in one creator and supreme being called *Pathian*[4] (literally translated as "holy father", holy in the sense of "pure"[5]), who, however, vaguely figured in everyday life but occupied no significant place in the "religious" (*sakhua*) practice. Though benevolent, he was believed to have little concern over human affairs.[6] He was conceived as the almighty who lived in a distant heaven from where he oversaw moral order in the world, directed human destiny,[7] and helped justice to reign. Although he was perceived to be unconcerned in human affairs, it was to him they "prayed" (or rested their fate) when in extreme difficult situations. When distressed, Mizos used to console themselves by saying, "there certainly is God" (*"Pathian a awm ang chu"*). When faced with baffling situation, they used to be resigned to their fate by saying, "let God's will be done" (*"Pathian thu thu ni rawh se"*). When they suffered injustice, they used to comfort themselves saying, "God knows it" (*Pathianin a hria a lawm*). Some think that there were traces of development in the *Pathian* consciousness as there appears to be increase in *Pathian*'s involvement in and concern for human affairs.[8]

Lesser than *Pathian* but of great benevolent power are a few spiritual beings. In his essay on "The Traditional Mizo Concept of God," C. L. Hminga lists some five or six names of benevolent spirit-beings. They are, *Pu Vana* ("heavenly grandfather"), *Khua-*

nu (mother cosmos or cosmic goddess), *Vanchung nula* (maiden in heaven), *Khuavang*, and *Lasi*.[9] To the list is also included the nameless spirit (or unknown spirit) whom one's ancestors worship in the *sakhaw*[10] worship which, some think, may not necessarily be seen as a god. Two of these, namely *Pu Vana* and *Vanchung nula* are so vaguely used in fables and *Pu Vana* may just be another name for *Pathian*. *Khuanu*, to whom the most important sacrifices were offered (see below), was often described as mother goddess and in other places also as *Pathian's* wife. Since *Khuanu* is a poetical word and "used only in poetry," there are suggestions that it may just be a poetical (and feminine) name for *Pathian*.[11] I am also of the opinion that it is possible to conceive *Pathian* and *Khuanu* as referring to the same being, one the feminine and the other the masculine name. One can also conjecture a family concept here with different beings representing different members of a family. *Pathian*, which literally means "holy father", as the father of the family, *Pu Vana* as either a synonym to *Pathian* or grandfather (i.e., father of *Pathian*), *Khua-nu* as his (*Pathian's*) wife and mother-goddess, and *Vanchung nula* as the daughter. Although not popular, there is a story of one by the name of *Vanhrika* who has been proposed to represent a son.[12] Unlike the more generic and common name of *Pu Vana* (heavenly grandfather) and *Vanchung nula* (a young heavenly woman), this one is a personal name and scarcely known.

Clearly distinct from *Pathian* but most powerful and active in human's lives are *Khuavang* and *Lasi*. *Khuavang* is a benevolent spiritual being who helped human beings in various ways. A powerful spirit of handsome stature, *Khuavang*, was regarded by most as slightly inferior to *Pathian*. A *zawlnei* or "one possessed" (which is used to translate "Prophet" in the Bible), was one possessed by a *khuavang*.[13] *Zawlnei*-s were highly revered and consulted for all kinds of help, including illnesses.[14] Somewhat close to *khuavang*-s in nature and power but having a specific area of functioning was *Lasi*. A *Lasi* is the owner of all wild animals and also presides over hunting. One who was lucky and successful in hunting was considered to be possessed, by or related to, a *Lasi* and was called *Lasi zawl* (possessed by a *Lasi*).

Malevolent Spirits

Like many other tribal groups in India and elsewhere, Mizos believed in the existence of a multitude of malevolent spirits. Saiaithanga listed at least eight different names of such ill-willed spirits, but the predominant and most troublesome are the *huai*-s. The others are *Chawm, Tau, Phung, Hmuithla, Maimi, Rau, and Khawhring*.[15] Some of these such as *Chawm, Phung, Hmuithla* appear to be specific names of *huai*-s. In his dictionary, the pioneer missionary to Mizoram J. H. Lorrain renders *huai* as "evil spirit" and "demon". The *huai*-s, commonly named *ramhuai* (jungle demon) peopled every part of the world, and they were believed to have favourite habitations, such as big trees, ponds, caves etc. In fact, the *huai*-s of such objects were identified with the objects themselves as their souls or spirits. Therefore, most animate and inanimate objects were believed to have spirits. If "animism" is defined as "attribution of soul to inanimate objects or natural phenomena,"[16] or simply as "plurality of spirits and ghosts,"[17] there are reasons to conclude that the Mizo religion was animistic. Several scholars in Northeast India objected to labelling the primal religion of the tribal people as animism. Such objections have been made because of the pejorative connotation attached to "animism".[18] Ironically, however, similar objections have not been raised against the use of other such derogatory terms as tribal.

Huai-s, which came to be commonly called *ramhuai*-s, were believed to be uniformly bad, and "all troubles and ills of life", including every form of sickness, were attributed to them.[19] Some believed that *huais* do not attack unless provoked, but humans continually and unknowingly encroached their habitation. Because of such encroachments, they attacked human beings causing all illnesses and even epidemics. Propitiatory sacrifices were offered to the *huais* both as community and as individual families. The belief was that *huais* could be appeased through sacrifices offered in the prescribed manner. This takes us to the discussion of sacrifices and sacrificial ceremonies in the Mizo religion.

Sacrificial Rites and Ceremonies

The sacrificial rites and ceremonies performed by Mizos can be classified under three families. The first of these were family community sacrifices seeking "divine" blessing and prevention from ill-health and other dangers. The second group was the various kinds of propitiatory sacrifices for sick individuals to appease and ward off *huais* who caused illnesses. The third one is *sakhua,* a family rite of sacrificial worship addressed simultaneously to the cosmic goddess (*khuanu*) and the guardian spirit worshipped ancestrally by a clan. The religious nature of the second group has been debated, and the performer called *bawlpu,* translated in the past as priest, has now been understood more accurately as a "medicine-men man"[20] or a "sorcerer."[21] In the other two groups of sacrificial ceremonies, the village priest, called *Sadawt,* performed the sacrificial acts. After a brief description of the first two, the third one will be dealt with in a relatively detailed manner as it has often been considered to be the core of Mizo primal religion.

The first group of sacrifices was the community sacrifices offered at certain occasions and seasons. Prominent among them were *Kawngpui Siam* (a means of seeking blessings on hunting), *Ramar Thih* (seeking protection from accidents at the time of clearing the forest for cultivation), *Fano Dawi* (to bless the rice crops of the village), *Khawkheng Thawi* (sacrificial prayer for rain).[22]

To whom did they offer these sacrificial prayers and ceremonies? It certainly was not to the evil spirits or demons, but to benevolent spirit or spirits. But it was never clear which spirit or spirits.

Every illness was believed to be the result of the displeasure of a *ramhuai* (demon). To appease as well as to ward off the demon, sacrifices were offered on behalf of the sick by a *bawlpu*. Either by checking the pulse of the sick person or by casting lots (by *zawlnei*), the identity (or name) of the *ramhuai* and the kind of animal sacrifice it demanded were first determined. As the offering was made, the *bawlpu* chanted his or her incantation asking the demon to leave and let go of the patient.[23] Surprisingly, the parts of the sacrificial meat offered to the *huai* were the most unwanted parts of the meat, and the remaining meats were consumed by the family, relatives and the *bawlpu*. There are various ways and means of performing this rite, and the number grew from decade to decade.

Were the sacrificial rites to the demons to be considered worship? Were these rituals part of the Mizo primal religion as some had alleged in the past? This has been a debated point. Two prominent Presbyterian pastors have written on Mizo religion and came to take opposing positions. Saiaithanga unequivocally stated that "Mizo religion was about worship of *ramhuais*" and Liangkhaia, in the same forthright manner (without reference to the opposing position or proponents), said that the Mizo *sakhua* (using the term as equivalent to religion) involved no worship of *ramhuai*. Liangkhaia limited his understanding of Mizo religion within the meaning of *sakhua*, which, as we propose here, was only a part of the religion. The issue here is what do we mean by "worship" and what does it include? Should religion mean practices only in reverence? Should we call propitiatory offerings made to evil spirits (who were neither revered nor respected) sacrificial worship? In a context where the link between worship and the Supreme God had not been established, one can argue that sacrificial worship need not necessarily relate to the revered being(s).

Sakhua in the Mizo Religion

As said above, it is easy to say *sakhua* "was" religion, but our contention is that *sakhua* was only part of the religion and therefore was "in" the religion. The limiting of Mizo religion to the practice of *sakhua* fails to do justice to the idea of religion in Mizo society. We have mentioned earlier that several writings on Mizo religion have confined the meaning of the religion in the meaning of *sakhua*. Liangkhaia is most candid on this matter, and has provided us with a clear description of the *sakhaw* practice. What was *sakhua* essentially? The word *sakhua*, according to Liangkhaia, was a combination of the two objects of worship in Mizo religion, which were *sa* and *khua*. Whereas *sa* was related to the clan-identity to which one is born, *khua* referred to the immanent protector and cosmic goddess *khuanu*. The former, in which the spirit of the ancestors' protector was invoked, was worshipped by offering pigs, and to *khuanu*, domesticated mythun (or mithan) was offered.[24] The offering here was not really a sacrificial offering in the sense of expiation or propitiation, but for the act of worship. Based on an interview with a former priest of Mizo *sakhua*, the research team of the Tribal Research Institute cautions us that *sa* and *khua* should not be separated too definitively as Liangkhaia does. The act of *sakhaw* worship was one, not two.[25]

Sakhaw worship was a costly affair. It consisted of stages of "worshipping" acts, each of which involved a sumptuous public feast. The initial less expensive ones were considered to be almost obligatory; the remaining stages in the series of worshipping feasts were optional. The higher the stage the costlier the act. The completion of all the stages placed one in the most coveted and respectable position in the society, called "*thangchhuah*," which also carried a promise of paradise or heaven (*pialral*) in the life after death. Whereas the ultimate aim appears to be *pialral* through the attainment of *thangchhuah*, the immediate aim which also served as the means to achieve such a position, namely public feasting, was to serve and bless the entire community. Thus, the *sakhaw* practice meant for invoking blessing was itself a blessing to the community. It was this benevolent aim of feeding the community that linked this type of *thangchhuah* (i.e., through *sakhaw* practice) with another *thangchhuah* called *Ram lama Thangchhuah* or *thangchhuah* in the hunting field. The second type of *thangchhuah* was set aside for those who achieved great hunting success[26] and have feasted the community numerous times. Interestingly, the second *thangchhuah*, i.e., *Ram lama Thangchhuah*, had no "religious" (*sakhua*) connection but carried the same promise of blissful life after death.

Life After Death

In the traditional Mizo conception of a human being, the soul (or spirit) continues to live even after a person dies. After death, the soul leaves the body through a crack in the skull.[27] After wandering around for about three months, the soul would then proceed toward the place of the dead. The *Rih* lake, which lies just beyond the eastern border of Mizoram in Myanmar, was believed to be the passage toward *mitthi khua* (or the village or dwelling place of the dead). After it passed through a special hill called *hringlang tlang* where it would turn back with sentimental longing for life and its dear ones, the soul would come to a place where it drank the water that ended the longing and would move on wearing the "flower of no turning back" (*hawilo par*). The route then would lead to a narrow gorge where a man named Pawla (Paul) stood with his pellet bow. He shot at everyone going to the village of the dead, and the shot with the egg-sized stone pellet was so painful that it would cause a tumour, which takes at least three years to heal. It was at this point that the route appears to have divided, one leading to the village of the dead (*mitthi khua*) and the other to paradise (*pialral*). According to a tradition, other than those who attained the *thangchhuah* status, young men who had sexual relations with three or more virgin girls or seven women, virgin women, and infants escaped Pawla's pellet.[28] The origin of this tradition, according to Lalsawma is rather weak and its genuineness doubtful.[29] In the *mithi khua*, the souls of the dead led a shadowy and depressing existence in a miniature form. According to one tradition, the soul later escaped from the village in the form of dew which would evaporate and vanish forever.[30]

Pialral (or the land beyond the "*Pial*" River) has been translated as Paradise. This is the place for the privileged few. The most popular expression is that those in *pialral* will be fed with husked rice, inferring that there will be no more toil and hard labour. Today, the word is used as a poetical equivalence to heaven. Would all those who escaped Pawla's pellet enter *Pialral*? Some suggest that they would,[31] and others even liberally suggest that everyone leading a good life during their lifetime will be admitted.[32] But the tradition is not clear on this. Those who attain *thangchhuah* status, as we have said, would surely enter the *pialral*.

From Primal Religion to Christianity – A Break or a Growth?

In the history of Christian missions in India, Christianity is a latecomer to Mizoram. The pioneer missionaries set their feet in Mizoram in the last decade of the nineteenth century. Astounding is the swiftness by which Christianity swept the Mizo community. It took just about half a century to convert the Mizo community to Christianity. By the time India achieved independence in 1947, all the Mizos in Mizoram and most Mizos in the surrounding areas (Myanmar, Manipur, Tripura, Bangladesh) had embraced Christianity. What made the Mizos easily accept this new religion? Some suggest that primal societies with relatively simple religious systems easily fall prey to the more sophisticated world religions.[33] This may be one factor, but there are other crucial internal reasons and processes that played significant roles. There are a few major internal factors for the Mizos' turn to Christianity. Firstly, the existence of some common religious practices and beliefs between the Judeo-Christian tradition and the Mizo primal religion, such as good and evil spirits, sacrifices, and life after death. The effective use of common categories in the Christianization of Mizos both by missionaries and native evangelists were crucial. Such utilizations of common features need not be done consciously, as they were often done subconsciously. This factor played a role not only in the process of conversion, but also in the establishment of the distinctive characteristics of Mizo Christianity. We will explore this factor, focusing our attention on the message and its reception in the early years of Christianity in Mizoram. Secondly, like most other communities who converted to Christianity *en masse*, the committed works of the early Christian converts was were a major factor in connecting Christianity with the Mizo worldview and in disseminating the Christian message. Thirdly, in the case of Mizo Christianity, revival movements played a significant role in both the conversion *en masse* and in the indigenization of Christianity in Mizo society. As I have published my research on the last two factors,[34] I will deal with them only in passing.

Points of Contact

For his research on the growth of Christianity in Mizoram, C. L. Hminga interviewed some first generation Christians who had converted to Christianity. In response to his question as to why they became Christian, he received three kinds of responses. "Many", he said, "replied that they became Christian because they feared *'hremhmun'*." *Hremhmun* literally means "place of punishment" and is used to translate "hell." The second group said that it was because they wanted to go to *Pialral* or *Vanram* (paradise or heaven) after death. The third group said they became Christian because it provided the way to be healed from sickness without sacrificing to the demons.[35] It is clear that the responses were formulated in indigenous thought forms and terms, and that one may also infer that there was a deliberate attempt to meet the socio-religious vision of the Mizos in the presentation of Christianity.

In the same interview, Hminga also asked this group of first generation Christians "what was the Gospel message they first heard." Only one person remembered the message well. This person, who later became a pastor, said the message he first heard from the first Welsh missionary D. E. Jones in 1899 was, "Believe on 'Pathian' Jehovah and worship him, then you don't need to sacrifice to the demons any more. Even when you die you shall go to 'Pialral'."[36] This again clearly was a message constructed exclusively for the Mizos responding to their religious aspirations and goals. The missionaries learned to preach in such "a language" through their experience of interacting with the people. By putting a new stress on the belief in *Pathian*, interpreting him to be active and loving and even calling for his worship, the other two life's concerns of the Mizos, namely healing of sickness and the (new) way to *pialral*, were addressed in a profound manner. Based on oral tradition passed down in history and from some early writings, Lalsawma formulates the most primitive preaching as follows: "In heaven lived *Pathian*, the creator of the earth, human beings, and all living beings. Those who live according to his will go to heaven and live happily, and those who do not will be thrown into the hell of fire, and will suffer pain forever."[37]

Centring-God in the New Faith

From Hminga's interview and Lalsawma's description, we see that while some socio-religious beliefs were reformulated, others were utilized with no significant changes. We make the following observations: First, *Pathian*, the supreme being, came to be lifted from its inconspicuous form of remoteness to the most eminent position in religious life. He was now identified with the biblical Jehovah, and his worship was called for. As discussed earlier, *Pathian* had no interest in the daily affairs of human beings and he was believed to exist in a remote, distant place. He played no role in the healing of illnesses nor in the life-after-death affairs. He appeared to expect no worship and needed no service from human hands. However, to say that the Mizo primal religious belief had no significant influence on the conception of *Pathian* in Mizo Christianity[38] would be a denial of the translatability of the Christian message. Their self-consoling words that "God knows" at times when Mizos suffered injustice was an affirmation of the omniscience of God, and their comforting words that "there certainly is God" in times of deep distress affirmed the omnipotence of God (*Pathian*). On this foundation was built the concept of a loving and caring God-Emmanuel who wants his will to be followed. As a loving and caring God, his will for the world and for each individual is good. The change and continuity in the God-conception both connect with the people's frame of reference and leave room for reinterpretation.

Secondly, the faith in and worship of *Pathian* was put up as a challenge to supplant the highly burdensome practice of sacrificing to the demons (*ramhuai*). As discussed earlier, costly sacrifices were offered to appease the demons in times of illnesses, but the practice had no connection with the supreme *Pathian*. The Christian message conjoined the two beliefs, lifted up *Pathian* by reinterpreting him to be an immanent God to be worshipped also for one's benefit. The fear of demons, who were believed to be the source of all illnesses and pains, was a major impediment for accepting the new religion. In his report of 1898, the first Welsh Presbyterian missionary to Mizoram, D. E. Jones, wrote: "The first difficulty which the Lushai [Mizo] raises against accepting Christianity is the danger that he [sic] will be killed by the Evil Spirits, and when it is said that Christians do not become the prey of the Evil Spirits, they say in answer that our religion does for us and theirs for them. Yet some are ready to believe in Christ if they will be kept from illness in so doing."[39] The fear of demons was an ultimate concern as it was a life-and-death matter. Protection was demanded as a condition for accepting the new religion. In supplanting sacrifice to demons with the worship of *Pathian*, the name of Jesus, the conqueror and son of *Pathian* was prominent as the conqueror of evil spirits. In some way, as we will discuss below, it was the fear of demons that helped in interweaving Jesus into the religious pattern.

Here, the "miracle" of modern medicine became a major support and a channel in accepting "the power" of the new religion to eliminate the fear of demons. From the name given to medicine, namely *damdawi*, which may mean curing through witchcraft (*dam* means cure or heal, and *dawi* means bewitch, practice of magic or witchcraft), it was clear that medicine was first understood and received religiously. In his 1899 report, the second Welsh missionary Edwind Rowlands wrote, "The medicine dispensed in the villages is eagerly taken, and they tell each other of the cures effected. This is supplanting sacrificing to demons."[40] By the time when the two pioneer missionaries came back to South Mizoram as missionaries of the Baptist Missionary Society in 1903, medicine had occupied an important place making way for the meaning of salvation and the saviour. The missionaries, J. H. Lorrain and F. W. Savidge, wrote, "Medicine is a great factor in winning the hearts of these people to the Saviour, and it becomes a real test of faith when a man is willing to give up sacrificing to evil spirits to cure his sickness and trust to the great Healer instead."[41] Most of these early missionaries received some basic medical training. Savidge had extra medical training and had made special arrangement with a chemist in Yorkshire to replenish his stock of the latest drugs, which proved to be extremely appealing to the Mizos.[42]

Thirdly, the belief in and worship of *Pathian* also replaced the difficult and costly *thangchhuah* we have discussed as the path to *pialral* (heaven). The belief in life after death was a major resource for missionaries to conjoin the beliefs of the two religions. The belief in the existence of two different and contrasting abodes of the dead further provided an important link between the two. The existent contrast between the two places was furthered in the Christian message when *mithi khua* was supplemented and subsequently supplanted by *hremhmun* (hell). Although *mithi khua* (village of the dead) was not hell, it provided the means to form the idea of hell in the Christian teaching of life after death. *Pialral* on the other hand came to be identified with the Christian hope of life after death right from the beginning. From the early days of Christianity in Mizoram, Mizo Christians related their Christian hope of heaven with the existing belief of *pialral*. As the interviewees of Hminga we have mentioned above said, the term and idea of *pialral* was used to express their hope for the life to come. In a number of hymns written by Mizos, the imagery path to *pialral* is utilized to describe the hope of life to come. In his classic book on the life, customs and ceremonies of Mizos published in 1912, J. Shakespeare, a well-known British colonial administrator in Mizoram, reproduced an account of "the world beyond the grave" written for him by a Mizo. The writer included a map, says Shakespeare, in which he (the writer) "inserted the Christian's village and their heaven, the road to which is under Isua (Jesus), while the roads to the … Mi-thi-khua are watched by Seitana (Satan)."[43] Shakespeare made a significant comment, saying, "This incorporation of the teaching of missionaries with the indigenous belief is not without interest, showing a broad spirit of tolerance in the author, who, without abandoning the faith of his forefathers, is ready to admit the truth of Christianity and its suitability to those who profess it…."[44]

In the village community of Mizo society, only the *thangchhuah* were given sure promise of *pialral* after death. *Thangchhuah* was a lifetime achievement of very few individuals who were exceptionally rich or were heroic hunters and warriors. This was for a very exclusive group of people. The belief in and worship of *Pathian* was presented as an alternative path open to all which eventually eliminated the other path.

"Christus Victor": An Interposed Christology

Whereas those religious categories and divine figures which had direct matching in the primal religion were easily understood as they provided direct points of contact between the new and the old religion, new and foreign elements or figures had to be introduced with utmost care. The introduction of Jesus Christ as the main divine figure appeared to be both appropriate and new. While representation of God in familial terms was appropriate, a son figure in connection with God (*Pathian*) was not known popularly. It was in this venture of introducing Jesus, the son of God, that the missionaries seemed to have stumbled the most. How was he introduced? From available sources, it appears that the name was interposed within the existing (now reformulated) socio-religious framework. Recounting the early preaching of D. E. Jones, missionary-historian J. M. Lloyd said, "the preaching was often misunderstood. Metaphors were taken literally. When missionaries spoke of being saved through the blood of Jesus, some enquired about the kind of magic there was in such blood. Mr. Jones' enthusiasm and the fact that, on every possible occasion he spoke of Jesus, puzzled many."[45] The entire monologue-preaching system of communication was new and Jesus, the content of the preaching, was foreign. When one compares this description with the preaching of the same missionary we have quoted above as recounted by a convert, one notices a clear change.

The writing of another missionary brings out the process of the development more revealingly. At the tenth anniversary of the Baptist Missionary Society work in South Mizoram (1913), one of the pioneer missionaries, J. H. Lorrain included, in his annual report a retrospective reflection of their early mission among the Mizos. He wrote,

> Twenty years ago, the name of Jesus had never been uttered by Lushai [or Mizo] lips.... Our first message, as soon as we could speak the language, was a Saviour from sin. But the people had [no] sense of sin and felt no need for such a Saviour. Then we found a point of contact. We proclaimed Jesus as the vanquisher of the Devil – as the one who had bound the "strong man" and taken away from him "all his armour wherein he trusted" and so made it possible for his slaves to be free. This, to the Lushais [Mizos], was "Good News" indeed and exactly met their great need.[46]

Jesus, the vanquisher of the demons, not only make sense to them, but also met the "great need" of the people, said the missionary. The content of the "belief on *Pathian*" included his great son, the conqueror of the demons. Finding the "point of contact" in Jesus the "vanquisher of the Devil" is most significant in making the Christian message meaningful to the Mizos. This point of contact is essentially biblical and most meaningful for the Mizo. It brings together the two worlds. The strong appeal of Christianity to tribal communities around the world can be attributed to a common worldview shared with the primitive world of Jesus. This is the world of spirits with supernatural powers. Comparing the Western worldview with that of Asian, Asian missiologist Hwa Yung convincingly asserts that the Asian worldview is "generally much more holistic, without the sharp separation between the natural and supernatural with its emphasis on the world of spirits and dead…."[47] As a warring people existing in a precarious situation whose whole understanding of pains and sufferings had to do with the anger caused by unseen spiritual powers, God, as well as his son Jesus, presented as the conqueror of these powers could be most attractive. Jesus the exorcist of the Gospels was the Jesus many tribal groups, including Mizos, could easily receive and accept.

If there is a place for a Saviour and a saving work to be achieved, it was not a salvation from sin or divine condemnation that the Mizos desired, but a Saviour and a salvation from the pains and misery caused by demons. For those who were convicted of the existence of hell, which was easily related to the pitiful "abode of the dead," salvation from hell in the life after death was favoured. Lalsawma's recollected description of the early preaching confirmed what Hminga's interviewees had stated, namely salvation from hell. In Lalsawma's words, an early Christian message was that "God sent his son to save us from going to hell."[48]

Although we have been using the term "sacrifice" in connection with the Mizo primal religion, the Christian idea of sacrifice as forgiveness of sin did not make sense to them at first. This was perhaps because the concept of sin and the accompanying conviction of guilt were foreign to them. Instead, the atonement theory of "*Christus Victor*" that "Christ—Christus Victor—fights against and triumphs over the evil powers of the world"[49] seemed to have appealed to them the most. The idea of God in conflict with evil powers, which has close resonance in the New Testament writings, provides a strong ground for understanding God and Christ for tribal people. Sharing the worldview of the New Testament, the exorcist Jesus of the Gospels continues to appeal to the people even to this day. The idea of sin and propitiation for sin, as well as justification by faith, eventually made sense to them.

Spirits, the Spirit and Mizo Christian Spirituality

Any talk on Mizo Christian spirituality cannot but begin with the experience of revival in the history of Christianity in Mizoram. Here we briefly highlight the impact of revival on the indigenization of Mizo Christianity.[50] Churches in Mizoram and one of their main progenitors, the Welsh Presbyterian Church, are revival-led Churches. The "Christianization" of Mizoram is to be attributed largely to the four major waves of revival in the first four decades of the twentieth century. The Sprit-imbued revival movements matched a people who believed that they were living in the world of spirits. What made the revivals so important for the Mizos was their spirit-centred religiosity. Not only did the revival movements help to convert the entire Mizo community into Christianity, but it also transformed Christianity to become indigenous to the Mizo cultural ethos. The indigenous expressions of spirituality in the form of three native elements were given birth by the revivals. These are: The use of a traditional Mizo drum and drumming for singing in Christian worship service, native Christian hymns sung to indigenous tunes, and revival dance in close consonance with an earlier native dance. Today, these three practices are firmly established within Mizo Christianity, symbolizing an integration of Christianity with Mizo culture.

Having perceived their world as one peopled by a multitude of spirits, the belief in the reality of the spirits continues to have a firm hold in the Mizo community. A popular perception as expressed in what has become a common phrase is that "Christianity has chased away the demons." Yung's words quoted above on the blurred frontier between the natural and supernatural with the emphasis on the world of spirits scrupulously describe the dominant ethos of today's Mizo Christianity. Christianity is a spiritual religion through and through, and therefore, a Christian cannot but be spiritual. It was this kind of spiritual emphasis that made one leading pastor of the Presbyterian Church lament that moral decay has been a result of such "otherworldly" spirituality.[51] In this connection, one dominant strand of Mizo Christian spirituality may be highlighted to conclude this section.

Spirituality in the Mizo Christian sense of the term is closely linked to the idea of having a mysterious relation or connection with the unseen Holy Spirit. In fact, it is the word for prophet (*Zawlnei*) that conveys this notion most clearly. As discussed earlier, *zawlnei* in the Mizo religion were those possessed by *khuavang* (one of the deities), and were regarded somewhat highly. The power of the possessor is believed to be discharged mysteriously to and through the possessed. The Mizo understanding of prophet and prophecy has been deeply coloured by this kind of spirituality. This is quite different from the Greek meaning of *prophêtês*, i.e., "one who speaks before others."[52] Revival movements were characterized by the strange behaviour of being controlled or touched by an unknown force of the Spirit. The mysteriousness and the unpredictability of the "Spirit's manifestations" have often been considered signs of the authenticity of the work of the Holy Spirit.

The "Missionaries"

Our descriptions and interpretations of the presentation and reception of the Christian message to, among, and by the Mizos may have left an exceedingly positive and sanguine image of the missionaries to Mizoram. The missionaries, as latecomers, did benefit from the experience of earlier missionaries of the modern missionary movement. Like many other missionaries of their time, they were committed to the cause of mission as they understood it, and executed their responsibilities and duties well, but nothing extraordinary was to be identified in their methods, knowledge or charisma. The contributions of the native evangelists, which have often been greatly overlooked, must be recognized in this regard.[53] The story of native Mizo works in the conversion of Mizo people to Christianity is one of the most amazing stories I have come across in the history of missions. Named *tirhkoh* (the term also used to translate "apostle" in the Bible) but referred to as evangelists by the missionaries, they worked alongside the missionaries, crossing frontiers before the missionaries. As early as 1903, i.e., four years after the first converts were baptized, the small congregation (independent of the Welsh mission which had supported one) had already appointed and supported four *tirhkoh* or evangelists from among themselves, and that number gradually increased.

One characteristic feature of conversion *en masse* in the history of Christianity in India is the strong indigenizing force at work in and among the converts. At the height of the massive movement toward Christianity, the missionaries easily lost the controlling rein. Subconsciously, the people brought in familiar symbols, their values and worldview, and integrated them into their new religion. This was the case especially during the revival movements in Mizoram. The number of missionaries in the entire Mizoram was never large at any moment. The role of native converts in the evangelization and indigenization can hardly be over emphasized. One popular notion is that early converts were normally advocates of change and anti-continuity, and thus, they tend to oppose indigenization. While this general observation is acceptable, it is also true that because their knowledge, values and ethos were bound within their own native worldview, their thinking and actions cannot but reflect indigenous ideals.

Conclusion

In summary, let me briefly highlight the main points we have proposed. What we do here is we reread a few selected portions of the/a Mizo Christian account in connection with the Mizo primal religion and religiosity. The role of primal religion has been demoted and undermined in the accounts of Mizo Christianity with the result that the distinctive characteristics of Mizo Christianity have not been properly recognized. The popular notion has been that the Mizos have converted to Christianity and that they have completely abandoned their traditional religion. By questioning the abandonment theory, I traced important features of the demoted primal religion to find a line of continuity into Christianity. Both in the reception of Christianity and in conceiving foundational doctrines of Christianity, Mizos had made good use of their primal religious worldviews and conceptions. This is not meant to overshadow the significance of changes and transformation experienced by the people in their conversion to Christianity. In fact, practices that continued were also changed significantly in their forms.

Grounding itself on the foundation of the primal religious views, symbols, worldview and beliefs, Christianity became established among the Mizos. While it utilized much of the beliefs and practices, it, however, left no stone unturned. It reinterpreted the beliefs and practices, changed the relations, lifted up some elements, pulled down others and embraced new figures and elements. The *Pathian* of a distant heaven, who vaguely figured in the primal religion, came to occupy the central place in Christianity, with the condition that this change of divine roles and relations carries the religious promises and aspirations of the primal religion. A new figure came to be introduced in the person of Jesus, the *Pathian's* son, who served as the means to achieve and realize the religious goals and vision, and appropriately became the focal point of the new divine figuration. The continuity from primal religion to Christianity appears to be strongest in the doctrine of the Holy Spirit, upon which the spirituality of Mizo Christianity came to rest.[54] Interestingly, prophets as *zawlnei* (being possessed by the Spirit) are of prime importance in connecting the human to the divine in the Spirit's world.

Endnotes

[1] Two clear examples are: Liangkhaia, "Mizo Sakhua," in *Mizo Zia-rang* (Aizawl: Mizo Academy of Letters, 1975), and Tribal Research Institute, *Mizo Sakhua (Kumpinu Rorel Hma)* (Aizawl: The Senior Research Officer, TRI, Mizoram, 1983).

[2] B. L. Nongbri, "Change and Continuity: An Analysis of the Interaction of the Khasi Traditional Religion with Christianity," in *Christianity in Indian History: Issues of Culture, Power and Knowledge*, eds. Pius Malekandathil, Joy L. K. Pachuau, and Tanika Sarkar (Delhi: Primus Books, 2016), 58-75.

[3] Emile Durkheim, *The Elementary Forms of the Religious Life* (New York: The Free Press, 1965, originally published by George Allen & Unwin Ltd., 1915), 22.

[4] Lalrinawmi Ralte has proposed that there were three supreme beings in the Mizo primal religion, namely *Khuanu*, *Pathian*, and *Khuavang*. (See Lalrinawmi Ralte, "Patriarchy and Christianity in the Mizo Church: A Feminist

Critiquel *Bangalore Theological Forum* 31 {July 1999}: 118). The idea needs evidential substantiation.

⁵ Zairema, "The Mizos and Their Religion," in *Toward a Tribal Theology: The Mizo Perspective* (Jorhat: Mizo Theological Conference, 1989), 39.

⁶ J. Shakespear, *The Lushei Kuki Clans*, Part 1 (Aizawl: Tribal Research Institute, 1975; Originally published in London, by Macmillan & Co., 1912), 61.

⁷ Zairema, 39.

⁸ Mangkhosat Kipgen, *Christianity and Mizo Culture* (Jorhat: The Mizo Theological Conference, 1996), 116.

⁹ C. L. Hminga, "The Traditional Mizo Concept of God," in *Toward a Tribal Theology: The Mizo Perspective* (Jorhat: Mizo Theological Conference, 1989), 46-51.

¹⁰ *Sakhaw* is the adjective form of the term *Sakhua*.

¹¹ Zairema, 39.

¹² I owe this information to my friend, the late Rev. Dr. R. Chhuanliana Colney. See R. Chhuanliana Kawlni, "Logos and Vanhrika: Rereading Johanine Christology from a Mizo Mythological Perspective, *Journal of Tribal Studies* 8, No. 2 (July-December, 2004): 54-76.

¹³ Saiaithanga, *Mizo Sakhua* (Aizawl: Maranatha Printing Press, n.d.), 3-4.

¹⁴ Ibid., 12.

¹⁵ Ibid., 5-7.

¹⁶ Zairema, 32-33.

¹⁷ Mircea Eliade, ed. *The Encyclopedia of Religion*, Vol. 1 (New York: Macmillan Publishing Co., 1987), s.v. "Animism, Animatism," by Kees W. Bolle.

¹⁸ A. Wati Longchar, *The Traditional Tribal Worldview and Modernity* (Jorhat: N. Limala Lkr, 1995), 9-10; Kipgen, Kipgen, 106.

¹⁹ Shakespear, 65-67.

²⁰ Zairema, 33.

²¹ Shakespear, 61.

²² Ibid., 26-27; Also see Shakespear.

²³ Saiaithanga, 28.

²⁴ Liangkhaia, 1-2. Domesticated mythan (or mithun, also named in some dictionaries as gayal) was the most valued possession in Mizo society.

[25] Tribal Research Institute, *Mizo Sakhua (Kumpinu Rorel Hma)* (Aizawl: The Senior Research Officer, TRI, Mizoram, 1983), 11-12. Hereafter TRI, *Mizo Sakhua*.

[26] A hunter is required to have hunted down the following wild animals: an elephant, a bear, a wild gayal, a stag (an adult antlered-deer), a wild boar, and a flying lemur. K. Zawla, *Mizo Pipute leh an Thlahte Chanchin*, Revised and Enlarged, 6th Edition (Aizawl: The Author, 1993), 35.

[27] Zairema, 40.

[28] Kipgen, 120.

[29] Lalsawma, *Kristian Thurin Zirna*. The Textbook of Adult Sunday School of the Mizoram Presbyterian Church for the year 1999 (Aizawl: Synod Literature and Publication Board, 1998), 306.

[30] Zairema, 40.

[31] Kipgen, 119-120.

[32] Lalsawma, 305.

[33] Stephen Neill, *A History of Christian Missions*. The Pelican History of the Church, Vol. 6. Second Ed. Revised by Owen Chadwick (Middlesex, England et al.: Penguin Books, 1986), 218.

[34] For my discussion on the role of native Christians, see Lalsangkima Pachuau, "Church-Mission Dynamics in Northeast India," *International Bulletin of Missionary Research* 27, No. 4 (October, 2003): 154-161. On role of revival movements, see Lalsangkima Pachuau, *Ethnic Identity and Christianity: A Socio-Historical and Missiological Study of Christianity in Northeast India with Special Reference to Mizoram* (Frankfurt: Peter Lang, 2002), 111-143.

[35] The interview was conducted in the summer of 1975 to the few first generation Christians in South Mizoram who were still alive then. See C. L. Hminga, *The Life and Witness of the Churches in Mizoram* (Serkawn: The Literature Committee, Baptist Church of Mizoram, 1987), 62.

[36] Ibid.

[37] Lalsawma, 307.

[38] This is the line of conclusion made by T. Vanlaltlani in her M.Th thesis. See T. Vanlaltlani, "The Experience of Pathian (High God) and Other Deities in Mizo Religion and Its Influence on Mizo Christians" (M.Th Thesis, Senate of Serampore College, 1990), 143-144.

[39] "Lushai Hills," in *The Report of the Foreign Missions of the Welsh Calvinistic Methodists (or Welsh Presbyterians) for the Year ending December 31st,*

1898 (Liverpool: Calvinistic Methodist Foreign Mission, 1899). Hereafter, cited as *FMCMPCW*. The annual reports of this mission, with some—historiographically uncalled-for—changes and adaptations, is now available as *Reports of the Foreign Mission of the Presbyterian Church of Wales in Mizoram, 1894-1957*, Compiled by K. Thanzauva (Aizawl: The Synod Literature and Publication Boards, 1997).

⁴⁰ "Lushai Hills," in *FMCMPCW 1899*.

⁴¹ *The Annual Report of BMS on Mizoram, 1901-1938* (Serkawn: The Mizoram Gospel Centenary Committee, Baptist Church of Mizoram, 1993), 8-9.

⁴² D. E. Jones, *A Missionary's Autobiography*. Compiled and Translated by J. M. Lloyd (Aizawl: H. Liansailova, 1998), 42.

⁴³ Shakespear, 62. Shakespear's book was first published in 1912, and in 1975 the Tribal Research Institute of the Government of Mizoram "re-published" it. Unfortunately, the TRI failed to mention the date of the original publication.

⁴⁴ Ibid.

⁴⁵ J. Meirion Lloyd, *On Every High Hill* (Aizawl: The Synod Publication Board, 1984), 24. The book was earlier published by the Foreign Mission Office of the Presbyterian Church of Wales, Liverpool (n.d.).

⁴⁶ Quoted from *The Annual Report of BMS on Mizoram, 1901-1938*, 93-94. Because there are some typographical errors in the quoted passage, a shorter quotation of the same passage (from the original source) by C. L. Hminga is used to correct the errors. This includes the corrective addition of "no" in the third sentence.

⁴⁷ Hwa Yung, *Mangoes or Bananas?: The Quest for an Authentic Asian Christian Theology* (Oxford: Regnum Books International, 1997), 3.

⁴⁸ Lalsawma, 307.

⁴⁹ Gustaf Aulén, *Christus Victor: An Historical Study of the Three Main Types of the Idea of the Atonement*, trans. A. G. Herbert (London: SPCK, 1953), 20.

⁵⁰ For a detailed discussion, see Lalsangkima Pachuau, *Ethnic Identity and Christianity: A Socio-Historical and Missiological Study of Christianity in Northeast India with Special Reference to Mizoram* (Frankfurt: Peter Lang, 2002), 111-143.

⁵¹ Lalsawma, "The Shaking of Foundations in Mizo Society," in *Mizoram Today*, Vol. 1, No. 2, January 21, 1975 (Aizawl: Directorate of Information, Public Relations and Tourism, Government of Mizoram), 13-17.

⁵² John L. McKenzie, SJ, *Dictionary of the Bible* (Bangalore: ATC, 1984), s.v. "Prophet, Prophecy."

[53] For further discussion on this subject, see Lalsangkima Pachuau, "Church-Mission Dynamics in Northeast India," *International Bulletin of Missionary Research* 27, No. 4 (October, 2003): 154-161.

[54] In another work, I have written more about the Holy Spirit. See Lalsangkima Pachuau, "Primal Spirituality as the Substructure of Christian Spirituality: The Case of Mizo Christianity in India," *Journal of African Christian Thought* 11, No. 2 (December 2008): 9-14.

PART 3

Christianity and Nationhood in Northeast India

CHAPTER 6

Re-Scripting a Christian History:

Christian Origins in Northeast India

The census report of 2011 shows that roughly 7.8 million Christians live in the seven states of Northeast India. [1] This represents just about 28 percent of the 27.8 million Christians in India as shown by the same report. The top five states with highest percentage of Christians in India are all in the Northeast, and in three of the seven states of Northeast India, Christians accounted for more than 70 percent of the state's population (87.93 percent in Nagaland, 87.16 percent in Mizoram, and 74.59 percent in Meghalaya). [2] However, Christians in Northeast India as a whole account for just 17.3 percent of the region's population. This low percentage is because Christian numbers are negligibly small in the two most populous states, Tripura and Assam. The state of Assam has just about 69 percent of the entire region's population, and only 3.74 percent of Assam's population is Christian.

Christianity has made inroads mostly among tribal communities while the non-tribal communities have largely resisted the missionary influence of Christianity. Popular perceptions have now largely followed the constitutional classification of the peoples in Northeast India into tribal ("scheduled tribes") and non-tribal people as discussed in the previous chapter. While the non-tribal groups consist largely of Hindu and Muslim communities, the larger number of the so-called tribal people of non-Indic ethnicities has embraced Christianity from their respective primal religions. Foreign missionaries were suspected to be clandestinely involved in the political secessionist movements in Nagaland (from the early 1950s) and Mizoram (from the mid 1960s to the mid 1980s) because Christians are in the majority in these states.[3] Missionaries were expelled during the heights of the secessionist movements in these states and have been barred from re-entry. With the multiplication of other violent political movements including among non-Christian communities in the region, such a suspicion has declined and is now confined mostly to *Hindutva* proponents.

Missionary historiography has been a point of contention, especially among Christian historians in India. The contention has been between hagiographic writings on missionary heroes at one extreme and the works of nationalist historians, some of which disparage missionaries and their works, at the other extreme. Some nationalist historians have gone so far as to depreciate the entire missionary enterprise and to conflate it with Western colonialism. In the context of India, nationalist historiography may be differentiated from indigenous historiography, which gives due attention to native viewpoints which are not necessarily nationalistic. Here we are claiming an indigenous Christian viewpoint which lies somewhere between missionary hagiography and a nationalistic attempt to eclipse missionary contributions. We recount the history of missions in the region by giving due appreciation to the Western missions and missionaries with a forthright attempt to recognize the contributions of native

Christians in the process. Our account will show that much of the evangelizing works were done by the early native converts under the oversight of the missionaries. Yet, it was the missionary who initiated and who shouldered the responsibilities. The simple fact is that without the missionaries Christianity would not have come to these—or for that matter many—parts of the world. Some passionate nationalist historians have overlooked such a simple fact.

Christians in Northeast India Today

The church is alive and active in most of the hill states of Northeast India today. Different tribal communities have adopted as well as adapted to the Christian faith. The Khasis, the Garos, the Nagas, the Kukis, and the Mizos have understood their societies to be Christian. From these largely "Christianized" tribal groups, evangelizing missions have proceeded to the neighbouring communities in Arunachal Pradesh, Assam, Tripura, and other parts of India. Sundays, as "the Lord's Day," are observed as religious holidays by most of these societies, and the community values and ethos are largely defined by their understanding of Christian teachings and ethics. Their worldviews have been Christianized to such an extent that most of them have closely related Christianity with their sense of ethnic identity. Young Christians from Nagaland are flocking to theological institutions around the nation while many Mizo Christians have left the comforts of their homes to serve as missionaries in different parts of India and beyond. From a population of a little over a million in Mizoram, missionaries are numbered in the thousands.

Being told that the religion they have come to adopt is a foreign religion, they seem to understand that their religious lives and practices are alien to their cultures. Such a perception would be easily dismissed by outsiders in seeing their distinct Christian lives and practices. In her ethnographic study of Mizo Christianity, Joy Pachuau has shown how deeply Christianity has penetrated Mizo society to make it a truly "Mizo Christianity."[4] Her ethnographic approach helpfully highlighted "the local rootedness" of Mizo Christianity in the face of "its alleged 'Western-ness',"[5] as she rightly stated elsewhere. Several historical studies, including my own, have corroborated this observation. The local rootedness of Christianity in the region may take different forms, and one may argue that Mizo Christianity has its uniqueness. But there's no question about the genuineness of Christianity among people who have embraced it as a people and have made Christianity their own. As the different chapters on the rapid spread of Christianity in Northeast India written by various authors testified,[6] it was through the making of the new faith as their own and adapting it in their cultures subconsciously that Christianity established itself among the Garos, the Nagas, the Khasis, and the Mizos.

The three largest denominations today are the Baptists, the Presbyterians, and the Catholic Church. Due in part to differences in determining membership, no comparable statistics can be compiled. Based on the Protestant missionary principle of "comity arrangement" of missions, Protestant mission societies which worked in the region divided the region among themselves based on linguistic lines and ethnic groups. The arrangement made it difficult for the Catholic Church to establish itself in some parts of the region. The arrangement has also resulted largely in drawing denominational boundaries across ethnic and linguistic lines. The Nagas, the Garos, the Assamese Christians and a few other ethnic groups in Assam are mostly Baptists of American origin. Most Khasis and Mizos of northern Mizoram together with a few ethnic groups in Southern Manipur and North Cachar hills of Assam are Presbyterians of Welsh Presbyterian origin.

Mizos in Southern Mizoram as well as other ethnic groups in Tripura are mostly Baptists of British and Australian origins. To the princely states of Manipur (the Imphal valley) and Tripura, which barred the entry of missionaries during the British period, Christianity made its inroads quietly yet powerfully through native Christian migrants and missionaries from the adjacent regions. The works of an independent mission agency called North-East India General Mission in southern Manipur from the second decade of the twentieth century is particularly noteworthy in this respect. The Christian presence in Tripura began with Mizo communities in the state, and from the 1940s, the Tripura Baptist Christian Union (TBCU) united Christians in the state. In recent years, missionaries from Mizoram, Nagaland and other parts of India have established churches in Arunachal Pradesh. Lutheran missions in what is now Jharkhand (formerly Bihar) and Bengal followed their members who migrated to Assam and established Lutheran Churches.

Excepting the small Anglican community in Assam and Meghalaya, churches in the region did not participate in the Church union negotiation that gave birth to the Church of North India in 1970. In its stead, under the initiative of Assam Christian Council (later renamed North East India Christian Council), mainline Protestant leaders were involved in a church union negotiation of their own from the mid 1940s to the beginning of 1970. But the negotiation did not yield an organic church union.[7] It did strengthen the bond among the churches in the council. Today, strong conciliar relations across denominational, ethnic and regional lines through the North East India Christian Council serve as the main channel of unity among Christians in the region. Some of the larger denominations which spread across linguistic and ethnic groups, such as the Baptist and Presbyterian, are also united through denominational councils. The Baptists of American Baptist origin are now organized under the Council of Baptist Churches in Northeast India (CBCNEI), and the Presbyterians of different regions and language groups are organized as the Presbyterian Church of India (PCI).

Accounts of Christian Origins and Developments

Notable missionary works had taken place in the nineteenth century only in the present day Meghalaya state, and much of conversion to Christianity happened in the twentieth century. By the beginning of the twentieth century, Meghalaya (divided into the Garo Hills district and the Khasi-Jaintia district), which had 70 percent of the Christians in the region,[8] was the only place where Christianity had made its presence felt significantly. Although, a good number of Assamese had converted to Christianity, their number was insignificant in relation to the overall population. Mission work made headway in other parts of Northeast India only in the twentieth century.

Assam and Meghalaya

At the invitation of David Scott, the first British Commissioner of Assam, the Serampore Mission started a rather small-scale mission work by opening a school in Guwahati (Assam) in 1929. The school was closed in 1836, by which time another school had already opened in Cherrapunji (now Meghalaya). Following the amalgamation of the Serampore Mission with the Baptist Missionary Society in 1837, the Cherrapunji school was closed and the mission was abandoned in 1837.[9] Around the same time, in 1836, the American Baptist Mission appeared in the north-eastern part of Assam with the intention of reaching the Shan people of southern China. With the failure to move beyond the region, the missionaries of the American Baptist Mission gradually turned their attention to the region and adopted Assam as their field in 1841.[10] Christian growth among the Assamese was slow and the missionaries were frustrated. The only sign of success in Assam was among the tribal residents.

Christianity was first brought into the Garo hills, not by Western missionaries, but by two young Garo cousin brothers, Omed Watre Momin and Ramkhe Watre Momin, who ventured out of their region seeking education and a better life. In 1847, Francis Jenkins, the successor of David Scott as the commissioner of Assam, opened a school in Goalpara near the Assam-Garo Hills border. A number of Garo boys were enrolled as students.[11] Among them were the two cousin brothers Omed and Ramkhe. After completing their schooling, the two parted, taking different jobs. Surprisingly, they read the same Bengali Christian tract entitled "*Apatti Nashak*" in their separate locations. Omed, who became a policeman in Guwahati in 1857, found a copy of the tract in a vacated mission bungalow he guarded.[12] Ramkhe bought his copy in Goalpara.[13] When Ramkhe came back to Guwahati to attend the Government Normal School and joined Omed, the two mutually shared their new-found religious knowledge through the reading of the same piece of literature. Upon further enquiry and learning, they were convinced of the truth of Christian teaching. In the process, they were helped by an Assamese convert by the name of Kandura Smith, who later became the first Assamese to be ordained as a pastor. At that time, Kandura took charge of the American Baptist Mission station in Guwahati. The two were baptized on February 8, 1863, in Guwahati by missionary Miles Bronson during his visit to Guwahati.

Immediately after their baptism, Omed and Ramkhe approached Bronson about sending a missionary to work among the Garos. With the dearth of missionaries and the unlikelihood of acquiring new missionaries, Bronson told them not to expect a missionary soon. After a year, the two decided to quit their jobs and return to their homeland to share their new faith with their people. With Bronson's blessings and small salaries, they went back to the Garo hills in May of 1864. [14] Faced at first with intense opposition, even threatening their lives, the two eventually drew interest which grew into a small community of believers. Omed's work gave birth to a Christian village called Rajasimla, which became the seat of the first Garo Church. Ramkhe first opened a school in Damra and later helped to establish a new Christian village, Nisangram. [15] When Bronson finally visited Rajasimla at the invitation of Omed in 1867, he was overwhelmed to find 26 persons wanting baptism. ten others were added the day following the first baptism event. The baptism of the new converts, the organization of the Rajasimla Church, and the ordination of Omed all took place during the visit. Missionaries were immediately transferred and new ones appointed to the Garo hills, among whom the most noteworthy were E. G. Phillips and M. C. Mason. The noted historian Frederick S. Downs calls these two "the real pioneer missionaries." [16] From the native viewpoint, however, there is no doubt that Omed and Ramkhe were the real pioneers. They were not called "missionaries" but were referred to as "missionary assistants." [17] But they did not assist the so-called missionaries; instead they led them. Henceforth, the church grew among the Garos.

The earliest Khasi converts were introduced to Christianity by Krishna Pal of the Serampore Mission (West Bengal) of William Carey, Joshua Marshmann, and William Ward. The converts were from the foothills of Khasi land (now part of Bangladesh), and were baptized in 1813. After the abandonment of the Serampore Mission's station in Cherrapunji, the Khasi and Jaintia hills (of today's Meghalaya) came to be adopted by the Welsh Missionary

Society,[18] which sent its first missionary, Thomas Jones, in 1841. As in other places of Northeast India, devising a written form of the language and formal education at the primary level became the preliminary and basic means of evangelization. The growth of Christianity was slow in the early years and opposition was often violent.[19] There were only twenty Christians at the end of the first decade (1841-1851).[20] The standard of church membership was high, and the missionaries were slow to baptize new converts.[21] The Church began to grow in the last two decades of the nineteenth century.

The commitments of early Khasi converts are worth mentioning. There were women converts in the matrilineal system of the society who lost their rights of inheritance, and prospective chiefs such as U Borsing of Cherrapunji sacrificed their political positions because of their conversion.[22] The zeal to evangelize their own people began early among the Khasis, which soon developed into the creation of the Home Mission at the end of the nineteenth century. By 1940, as many as 24 new churches were planted with more than 2500 new converts through the work of the Home Mission.[23]

Not only did Khasi evangelists greatly contribute to the evangelization of the Khasi-Jaintia hills, but also in cross-cultural evangelism. In the history of Christianity in Mizoram, for instance, the Khasi contributions were noteworthy. Along with the first Welsh missionary to Mizoram, D. E. Jones, was a Khasi evangelist, Rai Bhajur, who sacrificed a high-ranking government job and a good salary to serve in Mizoram at a minimal income.[24] During his two years of service (1897-1899) as an "evangelist" assisting missionaries, Rai Bhajur was said to be the most frequent visitor to a Mizo bachelor quarter called *Zawlbuk* in the central part of Aizawl where he met young men and taught them about

Christianity.[25] There were a few other Khasi Christians who came to Mizoram for secular works who made immeasurable contribution by witnessing to their Christian faith among the Mizos. Among them was a government contractor by the name of Sahon Roy. Residing mostly in the southern district of Mizoram, where there were no resident missionaries until 1903, but where people were relatively more receptive to Christianity, Roy was credited with playing a significant role in the early growth and organization of Christianity in the south. When the Baptist missionaries arrived there in March of 1903, they found 125 Christians, of whom 13 were already baptized.[26]

Nagaland

Various factors, including a promise of "harvest", conflict between some missionaries, and lack of response from Assamese, led to the drawing of attention away from Assam to Ao Nagas, one of the sixteen Naga tribes of present day Nagaland.[27] The names of Edward Winter Clark and his wife, Mary Mead Clark, have been associated with the pioneering endeavour among the Ao Nagas. However, the real pioneer who first landed among the Ao Nagas with the Gospel was an Assamese convert who has been referred to as Clark's "assistant." His name was Godhula, who was given the Anglicized Christian name Rufus Brown. After learning basic Ao language, Godhula visited Haimong village in the Ao territory without the permission of Clark in October of 1871. Being suspected of being a government spy, he was caught by Ao Nagas. His life was threatened and he was confined in isolation for three days.[28] Godhula then gained the trust of the people, established good relations, and after he was released he returned to village several times. In April of 1872, Godhula and his wife went and lived in Haimong village for several months, and when they came back to Sibsagar in November, they were accompanied by nine new converts who were baptized by Clark. The baptism of nine Ao Naga converts, followed by others within a month, marked the beginning of Christianity in Nagaland. Clark moved to the Ao land in 1876 and started evangelization work through preaching, schools, and literature work. He continued to utilize the "help" of Assamese and had 15 Assamese "assistants", starting with Godhula in the early evangelization work of the Ao Nagas.[29] The early years did not see much conversion, and the Christian life he introduced was not acceptable to the succeeding missionaries who, in fact, dismissed almost all the members of this early congregation to give way for a radical reformation of the church. The drastic reformation in the Ao church in 1894 considerably reduced the number of Christians. A renewal movement again came about through the work of a young native convert by the name of Caleph. Along with his Assamese friend Biney, Caleph led evangelistic preaching tours, which greatly helped the growth of Ao communicant members. The movement resulted in the recovery of the church, even leading to the formation of an association of churches.[30]

With Clark's motivation, other mission stations were opened among the Angami-Nagas, and for a brief period among the Lotha-Nagas. Although C. D. King, the pioneer missionary among the Angami-Nagas, who started his work from 1879, had the advantage of the British administration's protection and support, no visible fruit could be seen immediately. A third mission station was opened among the Lotha tribe in 1885. But Christian growth did not take place until the third decade of the twentieth century among the Angamis and Lothas. It was among the Sema tribe, largely through the initiatives of a few Sema converts and the works of Ao evangelists that another phenomenal growth of Christianity came about. A certain man of the Sema tribe by the name of

Ivilho attended the Mission School in Kohima and converted to Christianity around 1906. Through him Christianity spread, and by 1913 even the chief of a village was reported to have been converted.[31] In the furtherance of Christianity among the Semas and other tribes, Ao Christians made significant contribution. Through what Puthenpurakal calls "a chain of reaction," lay Ao evangelists carried on the work of evangelization, leading to what he calls "a mass movement" among the Sema people.[32] Due in part to administrative restrictions by the colonial government, missionaries themselves could not reach out to the hinterlands of the colonial stations. It was the Ao Christians who first reached out the Sema people at the behest of the missionaries. Evangelist Rev. Sübongwati (the first Naga to be ordained), interpreter Imnasüshi (who spoke Sema language) and evangelist Kilenzilu were known for their initiation of works among the Sema people.

By 1926 when the American Baptist Mission celebrated the golden jubilee of Ao-Naga mission, churches were planted in four Sema villages. [33] Ten years later, in 1936, mission work was extended into the Tuensang and Mon areas among what were then called "Border Tribes" with the appointment of Rev. Kijungluba, who worked with a school headmaster, Mayangnokcha. Although missionaries acknowledged them as "the hands and mouths of the missionary" in the new field, Bendangyangbang Ao is right in observing that all the credit for the planting and growth of the church in this area should be given to these two men. He said, "Essentially, the missionaries simply extended moral support [to them]."[34] Independent from these mission endeavours done at the behest of American Baptist missionaries, the *Ao Mungdang* (Ao-Naga Church Assembly) commissioned Semsalepzüng in 1926, who had been working among the Sangtam people in the region adjacent to Tuensang and Mon. Semsalepzüng founded the first church among the Sangtams in 1928 in the village of

Chari.[35] When the financial support for the Rev. Kijungluba was transferred from American Baptist missionaries to *Ao Mungdang* in 1936, all of the missionary works among the border tribes fell to the hands of the *Ao* churches.[36]

While the growth of churches among the Aos, which began from the first decade of the twentieth century, was gradual, the growth among Semas and Lothas, dating from the 1930s, was impetuous and spontaneous. The hard resistance by Angami people also began to break down in the 1930s.[37] The major growth of Christianity among these tribes, as well as the initiation and growth among other Naga tribes, began after the Independence of India in 1947, and continued after the missionaries left Nagaland in the early 1950s. The contribution of Naga Christians in the evangelization of Nagaland is enormous. As early as 1898, the missionary report on Ao-Nagas said "all our churches are now self-supporting."[38] From 98,068 in 1951,[39] the number of Christians in Nagaland rose to over a million in 1991,[40] and by 2011, almost 1.8 million. As said above, not only does Nagaland have the largest number of Christians among the states of Northeast India, the Christian percentage of 87.93 in 2011 (a drop from 89.96 in 2001) is the highest in India. The fact that the major expansion of Christianity took place in the second half of the twentieth century when all foreign missionaries had left Nagaland is a living witness to the role of Naga Christians in the evangelization of Nagaland.

Mizoram

The pioneer missionaries to Mizoram, J. Herbert Lorrain and F. W. Savidge, belonged to a private missionary agency called the Arthington Aborigines Mission, founded, funded, and directed by Robert Arthington, Jr.[41] The two reached Mizoram in January 1894 and worked for about three and half years. Due to differences with their sponsor, Robert Arthington in the goals for the mission,

Lorrain and Savidge offered the area to the Welsh Mission, which had earlier planned to adopt the district. The first Welsh missionary to Mizoram, David Evan Jones, who came with a Khasi "evangelist" U Rai Bhajur, replaced the Arthington missionaries in 1897. When the southern district of Mizoram was transferred to the Baptist Missionary Society, the two pioneer missionaries went back to Mizoram as the first two Baptist missionaries in 1903. The first baptized Christians received their baptisms in 1899 under D. E. Jones. A third mission society, an independent Lakher Pioneer Mission, came to work among the Lakher tribe in the southernmost part of Mizoram in 1907. The churches planted by this mission came to be called the Independent Church of Maraland.

As in other places of Northeast India, it was the first converts who made headway in evangelizing their people. One of the first two Mizo converts, by the name of Khuma, is said to have visited almost all the villages in Mizoram with a simple message of invitation to each individual he met and house he visited: "Believe in Jesus Christ."[42] In a letter dated November 17, 1902, Jones wrote, "Today six young men went out two by two, to the North, to the West, and to the East to preach the Gospel throughout the land."[43] By 1903, the small congregation appointed three evangelists (preachers) and supported them with a monthly salary of Rs.3.00 each. Two years later, two others were appointed, and the five divided all of northern Mizoram among themselves as their region of operations.[44] The five took upon themselves to ensure that each household in each of their regions heard the gospel and invited them to become Christians. Similar was the development in southern Mizoram, which had become the field of the Baptist Missionary Society in March of 1903. In his letter to his father dated April 23, 1903, one of the two Baptist missionaries, J. Herbert Lorrain, wrote, "Last Sunday was a red letter day for the Lushai Christians here. It was the occasion of the sending forth of two of their members as evangelists to the surrounding villages."[45] As a way of training and organizing these so-called "evangelists," the first theological school was started by Welsh missionaries as early as 1907.[46] The school developed into a theological college to train pastors. The spread of Christianity also came in large part by way of a neighbourly sharing of faith. Conversions happened in flocks through the revivals, producing animated Christians. Enthusiastic converts who could not contain themselves in mere worship went about, sometimes in groups, singing and preaching their faith to others. From such unorganized neighbour to neighbour passing of faith emerged the practice of itinerant preaching which became a dominant mode of spreading Christianity among the Mizos.

Mizos are known for their love of singing and the sharing of their faith. Through a few Mizo diaspora communities in the adjacent regions in Myanmar (Burma), Chittagong in Bangladesh, Manipur, and Tripura, Christianity began its presence in those areas. Starting in 1910, a group of Mizo evangelists, employed by a certain Watkin Roberts under the Thadou-Kuki Pioneer Mission, was sent across the border to Manipur and Tripura, becoming cross-cultural missionaries. The contributions of this independent mission society will be dealt with later. A series of revivals in the first four decades of the twentieth century became most instrumental in converting the entire Mizo ethnic group to Christianity. The revivals not only helped to convert all the Mizos to Christianity, but also indigenized Christianity, bringing about a distinctly Mizo Christianity.[47] Teams of lay converts enthused by the revivals went about sharing their revival experience with their fellow tribe members, spreading Christianity from village to village. In a matter of about sixty years, the whole of Mizo tribe is considered to have become Christian.[48]

Manipur, Tripura, and Arunachal Pradesh

The two princely states of the region during the British Colonial rule, namely Manipur and Tripura, did not welcome missionaries. While missionaries managed to enter into Manipur only with great difficulty, Tripura remained closed. William Pettigrew, the pioneer missionary in Manipur, was from the Arthington Aborigines Mission. He entered Manipur in February 1894 and started his work among the Meitei (the non-tribal residents of the Manipur valley) people. Political conditions later compelled him to move to the hills and he worked among the Tangkhul people, a Naga tribe in northern Manipur. Pettigrew changed his denominational affiliation from Anglican to Baptist and joined the American Baptist Mission, which adopted him as its missionary and Manipur as its field.[49] Slow and steady was the progress of mission work among the Tangkhuls. The early converts, including some from the Kuki tribes, then took their new faith to their people. Due to his active involvement in political and other secular activities,[50] Pettigrew was unable to do much mission work. Due to political restrictions, only a few other missionaries were permitted to enter Manipur, and the major evangelistic work was done by the native Christians. The first Kuki to become Christian was Ngulhao, who has been reported to have prompted the conversions of at least 334 persons. Similarly, the effort of the first Thadou Kuki convert, Nehseh, is said to have resulted in the planting of the oldest church among the Thadou Kuki.[51] The same was true with the Zeliengrong Nagas and Mao Nagas of northern and north-western part of Manipur.[52] Large-scale growth of Christianity among these tribes took place after the First World War.

As mentioned above, an independent missionary agency, called the Thadou-Kuki Pioneer Mission, founded by Watkin Roberts with the help of Mizo Christians, came to work in southern Manipur. This new non-denominational agency was "manned entirely by native workers" mainly from Mizoram as it established itself in the area.[53] When this new mission agency extended its work into the neighbouring states of Assam and Tripura, it changed its name to North-East India General Mission (NEIGM) in 1919.[54] Because of conflict and dissension within the mission and clashes with other Protestant missions, ,there was an allegation of a breach of the comity agreement and NEIGM could not continue its work. In 1922, the mission was suspended from the comity of Protestant Foreign Missions in Bengal and Assam.[55]

As stated before, the state of Tripura has the fewest number of Christians in Northeast India, mainly because it did not permit missionaries until 1938.[56] The earliest Christian presence in the state, and subsequent mission work, began with Mizo immigrations to the northern border area of the state in the early part of the twentieth century. While the state was closed to foreign missions, the pioneering works began with Mizo Christians settled in the state.[57] A missionary ("evangelist") supported by the Mizo Christians, started evangelistic work among one of the Tripuri tribes, called Darlong, in 1917. The North-East India General Mission (NEIGM) sent its missionary to work among the Mizo immigrants in 1918, and among the Darlong tribe in 1919. Other missionaries of NEIGM followed, and most of them became pastors and teachers.[58]

In the meantime the New Zealand Baptist Mission, which was working across the border in present day Bangladesh, succeeded in gaining the permission to work in Tripura in 1938.[59] Gathering a small number of Christians of about one hundred, mainly Garos and Kukis residing in the state, the New Zealand Baptist Mission formed the Tripura Baptist Christian Union (TBCU) in December 1938.[60] Until the last missionary left Tripura in the early 1970s, TBCU was led by missionaries of the New Zealand Baptist

Mission. The Darlong Church joined TBCU in 1940,[61] and the Mizo Church, then called Jampui Presbytery, joined in 1944.[62]

The present Arunachal Pradesh, known in the past as North East Frontier Agency, has a long but insignificant interaction with Christian mission activities. Its geographical remoteness, ethno-linguistic diversity, and difficult accessibility for outsiders have prevented it from significant interaction with outsiders, including Christian missions. Consequential mission work, mainly by Christians from other states of Northeast India began in the 1960s, and the 1970s saw signs of significant Christian presence in the state. Through the works of native missionaries from other states of Northeast India, Christianity saw growth from the 1980s. As shown above, by 2001, nearly 19 percent of the state's population had become Christian.

The Roman Catholic Church in Northeast India
Unlike Protestant missions, the Roman Catholic Church in Northeast has no particular territory of operation. The Catholic presence in the Northeast dated the earliest, but the early contacts and presence were temporary in intention and nature. The first missionary society assigned specifically for the region, the Foreign Missionaries of Milan (PIME), came to the region briefly in 1872, but due to a jurisdiction dispute, no tangible work was done. In 1889, the region was re-assigned to the German Society of Catholic Education, popularly known as Salvatorians,[63] who began "Catholic missionary work proper"[64] in the region. During the First World War, the German Salvatorians were repatriated and the work was entrusted temporarily to the Belgian Jesuits (1915-1922) until the charge was handed over to Salesians of Don Bosco in 1922. The Salesian Brothers were joined by Salesian Sisters in 1923.[65]

While the numerical growth of Christians was slow under the Salvatorians, the pace of growth began to pick up with the Jesuits, and there was major growth in the first decade of the Salesians' work. Until the Independence of India, Catholic mission work was confined almost exclusively to present day Assam (or the Assam plains) and Meghalaya. Spectacular growth has been experienced by the Catholic Church in Northeast India since the Independence of India. Some new Religious Orders joined the effort strengthening the work together with diocesan clergies. From about 70,000 in 1945, the Catholic community reached 700,000 in 1990.[66] From the Assam plains and Meghalaya, the Catholic Church soon moved out to Manipur and Nagaland where it has been enjoying rapid growth.

Conclusion

If one is to give an overview of how Christianity spread in Northeast India, it may be said that the missionaries initiated the movement by introducing Christianity to a few individuals, and the native converts spread it. If the missionaries were seen to be the leaders and the native converts the "assistance" as they often were named, the reverse was also true. In some of the most critical instances, it was the "native assistants" who led the missionaries to new territory and helped them make sense of what Christianity means for the people.

The history of Northeast India after the Independence of India has been plagued by various political insurrections.[67] With a variety of political demands, a number of so-called insurgent groups have revolted against the government of India. From state to state, foreign missionaries were expelled and banned as they were suspected to have played clandestine roles in these movements. No foreign missionary is permitted in the region since the early

1970s. This turn of event has challenged, and even compelled, the churches to continue and enhance indigenous missionary endeavours. The missionary zeal displayed from the beginning received new impetus as concerted missionary efforts among the churches came to be made after foreign missionaries left the region. Much of the continuing expansion of Christianity in the region, and later in other parts of India, came through the missionary works of the Christians of Northeast India.

Endnotes

[1] The seven states are Assam, Arunachal Pradesh, Meghalaya, Nagaland, Manipur, Mizoram, and Tripura. Although quite close in territorial and cultural proximity, Sikkim has not been included.

[2] "Christian Religion Census 2011," https://www.census2011.co.in/data/religion/3-christianity.html (last access: Aug. 13, 2018).

[3] Jawaharlal Nehru, the first Prime Minister of India, once wrote: "Just when a new political awareness dawned on India, there was a movement in North-Eastern India to encourage the people of the North-East to form separate and independent States. Many foreigner[s] resident in the area supported this movement" (Nehru 1973: 4). Most of the foreigners residing in the area were missionaries.

[4] Joy L. K. Pachuau, *Being Mizo: Identity and Belonging in Northeast India* (Oxford: Oxford University Press, 2014), 136-158.

[5] Joy L. K. Pachuau, "Christianity in Mizoram: An Ethnography," in *Christianity in Indian History: Issuers of Culture, Power and Knowledge*, eds. Pius Malekandathil, Joy L. K. Pachuau, and Tanika Sarkar (Delhi: Primus Books, 2016), 47.

[6] Krickwin C. Marak, "Christianity among the Garos," J. Puthenpurakal, "Christianity and Mass Movement among the Khasis," O. L. Snaitang, "Christianity among the Khasis," A. Wati Longchar, "Christianity among the Nagas," and F. Hrangkhuma, "Christianity among the Mizo in Mizoram," in *Christianity in India: Search for Liberation and Identity*, ed. F. Hrangkhuma (Delhi: ISPCK, and Pune: Centre for Mission Studies, UBS, 1998): 155-311.

[7] J. Fortis Jyrwa, "Church Union Movement in North East India – A Historical Perspective," *Church, Ministry and Mission: Essays in Honour of K. Imotemjen Aier*, ed. Renthy Keitzer (Guwahati: CBCNEI, 1988), 58-71.

[8] Ibid., 80.

[9] Morris, *The History of the Welsh Calvinistic Methodists' Foreign Mission,* 72-75; Snaitang, *Christianity and Social Change in Northeast India,* 67.

[10] Sangma, *History of American Baptist Mission in North-East India (1836-1950),* Vol. 1., 30-45.

[11] Ibid., 188.

[12] Downs, *The Mighty Works of God,* 48.

[13] Carey, *The Garo Jungle Book,* 68, quoted by Marak, "Christianity among the Garos," 162.

[14] Downs, *The Mighty Works of God,* 49-50.

[15] Phillips, "Historical Sketch of the Garo Field," in *The Assam Mission,* 56.

[16] Downs, *The Mighty Works of God,* 53.

[17] Phillips, "Historical Sketch of the Garo Field," in *The Assam Mission,* 56.

[18] This was the original name given in 1840, and the name was changed to Welsh Calvinistic Methodist's Foreign Missionary Society in 1843 (hereafter "Welsh Mission").

[19] Downs, *History of Christianity in India,* 73-74.

[20] Puthenpurakal, "Christianity and Mass Movement among the Khasis," 202.

[21] Morris, 91.

[22] Ibid., 242, Downs, *History of Christianity in India,* 73.

[23] Jyrwa, *The Wondrous Works of God,* 38.

[24] Snaitang, "Christianity among the Khasis," 242.

[25] Vanlalchhuanawma, *Christianity and Subaltern Culture,* 124.

[26] Ibid., 122.

[27] Puthenpurakal, *Baptist Missions in Nagaland,* 57-62.

[28] Sangma, *History of American Baptist Mission in North-East India,* Volume 1, 222.

[29] Puthenpurakal, *Baptist Missions in Nagaland,* 72.

[30] Downs, *The Mighty Works,* 115-116.

[31] Philip, *The Growth of the Baptist Churches in Nagaland,* 104.

[32] Ibid., 104.

[33] Bendangyabang Ao, *History of Christianity in Nagaland,* 47-48.

[34] Ibid., 50.

[35] Ibid., 51.

[36] Ibid., 53.

[37] Downs, *History of Christianity*, 108.

[38] Quoted by Puthenpurakal, *Baptist Missions in Nagaland*, 116.

[39] Downs, *History of Christianity*, 108.

[40] *Census of India 1991*, Series-1 India, Paper 1 of 1995, *Religion*, xvii.

[41] For a biography of Robert Arthington Jr. and a brief story of the Arthington Aborigines Mission, see Lalsangkima Pachuau, "Robert Arthington, Jr. and the Arthington Aborigines Mission," 105-125.

[42] Saiaithanga, *Mizo Kohhran Chanchin*, 16.

[43] Quoted in Lloyd, *History of the Church in Mizoram*, 57.

[44] Lalchhuanliana, *Mizoram Presbyterian Kohhran Chanchin*, 74-75.

[45] *BMS Log Book*, BCM Archive, Serkawn, Mizoram, quoted by B. Thangchina, "A History of the Development of Mission and Evangelism," 24.

[46] Lalchhuanliana, 75.

[47] For a detailed treatment of the contributions of revivals in the making of Mizo Christianity, see Pachuau, *Ethnic Identity and Christianity*, 111-143; For a detailed chronicling of the revival movements, see Vanlalchhuanawm, *Christianity and Subaltern Culture*.

[48] Saiaithanga, 21.

[49] Dena, *Christian Missions and Colonialism*, 33-35.

[50] Ibid., 37, 39.

[51] Vaiphei, *Advent of Christian Mission*, 63-65.

[52] Ibid., 68-82.

[53] Dena, 51.

[54] For a detailed treatment of the NEIGM, see Vaiphei.

[55] Lal Dena., 53.

[56] Eade, "Golden Jubilee – Tripura Baptist Christian Union," 10-12.

[57] Lianthanga, *Tripura a Kohhran lo din tanna leh Chanchintha a darh zel dan*, 4-6.

[58] Ibid., 8-23.

[59] Eade, 12.

[60] Hnehliana, "Tripura Baptist Christian Union," 59.

[61] Lianthanga, 7.

[62] Eade, 2.

[63] Kottupallil, "A Historical Survey of the Catholic Church in Northeast India," 31-35.

[64] Downs, *History of Christianity*, 92.

[65] Kottupallil, 36-53.

[66] Downs, *History of Christianity*, 120.

[67] For further study on insurgency and Christianity in Northeast India, see Pachuau, *Ethnic Identity and Christianity*, 29-58, 145-175.

CHAPTER 7

Nationhood and Ethnonational Identity in Northeast India

When the Nagas first organized a movement for independence from India in the 1940s and 1950s, they clearly understood themselves as a "nation", and named their organization the "Naga National Council." Similarly, the independence movement in Mizoram from the mid 1960s also employed the concept of nationhood, calling the party, "Mizo National Front." Do the Nagas and the Mizos constitute a nation? When referring to the Naga National Council, an American scholar, R. A. Schermerhorn, inserts "[sic]" between "National" and "Council"[1] to signify that the use of "National" is erroneous or at least awkward. By this, he indicates that the Naga people do not really qualify as calling themselves a nation. This raises the whole issue of what a nation is, and consequently what is meant by nationalism. Nation can be understood in various ways. Whereas the modern concept of nationalism is closely associated with the concept of nation-state or what some called "secular nationalism," there are other ways of understanding nationalism outside the nation-state framework. Some of these became foundations for the construction of nation-states. Among the most common notions of nationalism are "cultural nationalism,"[2] "religious nationalism,"[3] and "ethnonationalism."[4] While Schermerhorn seems to understand the nation-concept purely in terms of a "nation-state" and consequently denies nationhood to the Nagas, I'd argue that the Nagas, the Mizos and other minority groups have understood themselves as a nation in the sense of ethnonationality and have sought to realize nationhood politically on the basis of their ethnic identity. The concept of "ethnonationalism" as the "pristine sense of nationalism,"[5] defines the self-understanding of the ethnic groups in Northeast India in the various forms of their struggle for identity.

By ethnonationalism, we refer to the political self-consciousness of the people based on their common cultural identity. Carmen Abubakar defines ethnonationalism as "Ethnic groups claiming to be [or to possess] nations and states in the past or that have the potential of becoming [nations or states and] are now demanding and asserting these claims as (historic) rights to self-determination for local autonomy or independence."[6] Today, there are "two models of nationalism that are in interaction and contention in many parts," says Sri Lankan social anthropologist Stanley Tambiah of Harvard University. One of these is "ethnonationalism" and the other is "nationalism of the nation state."[7] Broadly speaking, what other writers refer to as "religious nationalism" and "cultural nationalism" can be encapsulated within the concept of ethnonationalism. Tambiah helpfully delineates the political history of most of the developing nations into three phases.[8] The first phase is the "decolonization" period, which began in the 1940s and continued till the 1970s. The second phase, which began in the 1950s, was "the phase of optimistic nation-building." The stress on nation-building, he says, "down played . . . internal diversity and cleavages [within the new nations] in favour of the primacy of nation state."[9] The optimism and suppressive characters of nation-building in the second phase came to be challenged "and even reversed ... by the eruption of ethnic conflicts" in the third and the present phase of ethnonationalism. The phase of ethnonationalism, he says, is characterized by "regional or subnational reactions and resistances to what is seen as an over-centralized and hegemonic state."[10] In the case of the Nagas, the Mizos and others in Northeast India, the very notion as well as the movement of ethnonationalism clearly reflects a crisis of identity. The ethnonational self-understanding displays the experience of tension, being strained between ethno-cultural identity and political nationality.

Crisis of Indian "National" Identity in Northeast India

The multi-ethnic and multicultural setting of India and India's struggle to define its nationhood since the nationalist movement provided a fertile soil for the development of ethnonationalism and other forms of identity-quest. Closely linked to, and in some way encapsulated in, the idea of ethnonationalism is a more popular political terminology called "regionalism," which is prevalent in many parts of India, especially along linguistic lines. We may say that many parts of India have been pulled asunder by regional and ethnonational feelings and movements. Because it has not settled the notion of its identity in a manner convincing to all the people-groups within, India as a "nation" also suffers from an acute identity crisis. As G. Aloysius has rightly noted that Indian nationalism, so far, has failed to construct the nation in India.[11] While the dominant Indic culture at the centre continues its quest for self-identity on the basis of its religious and cultural identity, those on the periphery react to such potentially hegemonic and oppressive movement. Although existing as a nation-state for more than half a century, India has been struggling to find the central integrative force that can bind Indians together as a "nation."

Political struggle to define the basis of the nation between its socio-religious identity and its constructed secular nation-state identity occupies much of independent Indian history. The present day *Hindutva* movement is an attempt to find the religio-cultural basis of the nation of India. The crisis of identity at the centre reverberates onto the periphery, and the struggles on the periphery at times have turned very grievous.

Being ethnically different and often being depreciated for one's distinct identity in itself is a hard experience. When the centre shifts the integrative principle of the nation between secular nationalism and suppressive religious nationalism and displays deep uncertainty, those at the periphery feel their sense of identity to be extremely vulnerable. Such a crisis intensifies the identity consciousness of minorities and their sense of vulnerability forces them take defensive postures. Northeast India has seen its fair share of conflicts generated by this minority identity crisis.

Roots of the Problem of "National Identity" in the Northeast

Various factors contribute to the problem of being Indian for north easterners. The racial and cultural difference is conspicuous, yet the problem is not only in the people of the northeast themselves. Here we identify two major roots.

The Betwixt and Between Identity of the People of Northeast India

Geographically and racially, the region of Northeast India is situated between the two great traditions of Indic Asia and Mongoloid Asia. This geographical-cultural condition of "in-betweenness" is a significant factor for the crisis of identity. It was only from the British period that the entire region came to be associated with India politically.[12] Many leaders of the present day insurgents or "underground outfits" of the region may argue that the political integration of the region to India was done without taking the people's situation and sense of identity into consideration. There was not careful processing to integrate the people's sense of identity into India. The lack of cultural relatedness, especially of the "tribal"[13] culture, weakens the new political association, and the racial and cultural difference, thus, came to play a vital role in defining their separate self-identity. To answer the question "who are we?" most North easterners are caught between the racial-cultural definition and the politico-administrative definition of their identity. Whereas they are politically Indian—and thus at one with Indic Indians, they are racially and culturally eastern Asians of Mongoloid racial stock. The consciousness of the two differing identities is pulling the people and shakes political loyalty. The situation is worsened by the complex nature of Indic culture with which they have been—out of political necessity—associated. The problem of acceptance on the part of Indic culture with its caste-ridden social system, and the problem of identification on the part of the North easterners because of the underlying cultural and racial difference underpin the identity problem. These two underlying problems may be dealt with separately.

Sanskritization

When one talks about cultural plurality in India, since their traditional cultures share little or no commonality with the rest of India, the case of the "tribal" people in Northeast India is especially acute. To address the identity crisis in the region, one has to bear in mind the cultural plurality of the Northeast in general and the sharp difference between the people assimilated into Indic culture and the unassimilated "tribal" people in particular. Out of constant interactions, cultures influenced each other and developed commonalities. While the Indic-sanskritic culture of India is as a foreign culture as any alien culture is for some parts of the region, there are also areas where it has been at home for centuries. I contend that the assimilation of people into the Indic culture, mainly through sanskritization, became a defining factor for what is "tribal" and "not tribal" in the identity of the people of the region today. By sanskritization, we refer to the gradual processing of changing cultures toward sanskritic (or Indic) culture of the Hindu society.

What Ananda Bhagabati calls the distinctive "geo-ethnic character"[14] of the Northeast is helpful in clarifying the multicultural nature of and the cultural differences between the people. About three quarters of the region is covered by hilly terrain and one quarter is made up of the four plains areas of Assam's Brahmaputra and Barak valleys, the Tripura plains, and the Manipur plateau. Those in the thinly-populated hill areas are mostly the people now called "tribals;" and in the fertile plains and plateau reside mainly the "non-tribal" people, who comprises more than 80% of the total population. In recognizing the cultural foreignness of the "tribal" people of the hill regions, we should keep in mind that the sanskritization of the plain areas has been going on for centuries. F. S. Downs is right in pointing out that until the coming of British rule in the early nineteenth century, the entire region was never linked politically with any major Indian political power,[15] while the cultural link of some plains areas with the Indic culture dates back centuries. The *Mahabharata*[16] already mentioned Assam, calling it Pragjyotisha, and a reference to Kamrupa-Pragjyotisha is also found in the *Kalika Purana* and the *Yogini Tantra*.[17] R. N. Mosahary believes that "the Aryan intrusion" in the Brahmaputra valley of Assam might have begun as early as "one or two centuries before Christ."[18] The sanskritization or Aryanization of the indigenous people of Assam, the bulk of whom are of mongoloid race[19] reached its climax in the sixteenth century[20] when Hinduism became the most dominant religion and sanskritic Assamese replaced the native Ahom language. The Tipras, the indigenous people of Tripura, close kin of the Cachari-Bodos of Assam, have also been also Hindus for quite some time.[21] In the case of the Meiteis of Manipur, although there are claims of Hindu influence as early as the seventh century, the large-scale spread of Vaisnava Hinduism of Caitanya school began only at the end of the seventeenth century.[22] Around 1705, the Rajah of Manipur officially adopted Hinduism as the state's religion. Unlike in Assam, the Meiteis retain their native Tibeto-Burman language and do not follow a number of traditional Hindu practices, such as child marriage, the inhibitions against divorce and widow re-marriage, and the supremacy of Brahmin as well as caste hierarchy.[23]

Thus, the level of assimilation of the people into the Hindu religion and Indic culture differs from people to people or tribe to tribe. Whereas the Hindu-Assamese—who are relatively inculturated Hindus with some indigenous festivals and practices of their own—became sanskritized to the level where the people lost their native language and adopted many imported practices, the Meitei-Hindus retain many more indigenous practices and traditions within their adopted religion. The Hinduization of the region was limited to the plains areas, as Indic culture never reached the hill regions. Until the imposition of British rule in the nineteenth century after the treaty of Yandabo (1826), the hills were isolated and were preserved from the onslaught of sanskritization. Their cultural foreignness to the Indic cultural system clearly marks off the hill "tribes" from the rest of Indians. Is the non-Indic-ness the mark of "tribal" identity in the Northeast?

Ethnonationality and Political Conflicts

In the political parlance of India today, the Northeast region has come to denote ethnic differences. In the minds of the national majority, it has been associated ethnopolitical movements. Since India's independence in 1947, we have not seen a single decade of calm political atmosphere in the region. Instead, each of the first five decades witnessed new movements of political unrest, most of which turned to violent revolutions. One need not make a substantial argument to show that these movements have their origin in the ethnonational understanding of the identity. Insurgency, an extreme form of ethnopolitical upsurge, has rocked five of the seven states at one time or another, and the remaining states have also been highly poised for similar movements. Nibaran Bora's words in the early 1990s depicted the situation of the first fifty years of India's independence very well:

> Insurgency took roots in Nagaland and Manipur in the early fifties, immediately after the establishment of the Republic [of India], those in Mizoram, in the sixties, in Tripura in the seventies, while in the case of Assam it has arrived in the eighties. Meghalaya and Arunachal [Pradesh] are just now menacingly militant, not yet insurgent though, Karbi Anglong [district of Assam] too is equally poised.[24]

The inward-looking self-definition of identity as an ethnonational entity now not only affects the people's relations with "the outsiders," but also the inter-ethnic groups' relations within the region. The expectation of achieving economic and political liberation on the basis of ethnic groups have led to feuds between the people groups within the region. Although a common enemy is still strongly felt to be "the outsiders," in the attempts to define one's ethnonationality, and in the struggle for "autonomy" and liberation, the more powerful neighbouring ethnic groups came to be identified as obstacles. The Naga-Kuki clash in the 1990s is a good example. In identifying these regional issues, we should be cautious about not making it a mere regional issue. Although there may be more factors to be identified for ethnocentric politics in Northeast India, it is not endemic just to the region. The social and political climate of the larger Indian context is fertile soil to crystallize minority groups as political entities. What we may call "ethnocentric politics" in Northeast India corresponds to "communal politics" in the larger national context of India. The evils of communalism produced by various factors, including the national policy of using a language group to form a state and the obstinate caste hierarchical relations among communities, have been piercing Indian politics as a nation-state.

"Tribal" Identity

What is tribal about the "tribal" people in India? What tribalizes them to assume a distinctive "tribal" identity against the non-tribal people? These are pertinent questions to analyse the meaning and implications of the nomenclature. We need not spend time in discussing the pejorative meaning of the term "tribal", such as backward, irrational, and primitive.[25] In this section, I will offer my critique of the use or imposition of the identity called "tribe" or "tribal." It is not my intention, however, to critique the nomenclature for its own sake, or to determine whether or not the pejorative term is redeemable. In critiquing the nomenclature of "tribal," my intention is to highlight the fact that the very choice of the term by the nation's authority is an act of marginalization which also reveals the oppressive structure behind this imposition of a depreciative identity on a people. In other words, the very use of the term reveals the intent to dominate and oppress the people on whom the nomenclature is imposed. I am aware of the fact that in Northeast India, there are a number of "tribal" scholars who unquestioningly accept the nomenclature, and some find what is tribal in their tribal identity. I am not convinced by such "findings". What M. Horam says about "tribalism" of the Naga people[26]—which he seems to think is distinctive to the Nagas among the Northeast "tribals"—also prevails under the rubric of "communalism" of most Indian societies, as I have indicated above. I contend that the creation of tribalism is artificial; it is done for the convenience of the administrative system that is thoroughly influenced by the caste stratification mind-set, and politically and culturally controlled by the caste Hindu society. On top of all, this artificially constructed identity resulted in the intensification of the already existing identity crisis of the people in Northeast India.

Let me pick up the issue of Hinduization or Sanskritization from where I left off. As much as westernization through Christianity and the western educational system can be seen to have uprooted the people from their cultural soil, it must be noted that Hinduization had also uprooted the people from their traditional culture. If Christianity is to be blamed for the modernizing changes that have "civilized" and thereby de-tribalized the tribal people, the same allegation can be levelled against Hinduism. Regarding the Hinduization process we have described above, Ramesh Burgohain rightly commented that it had de-tribalized the formerly tribal people. The Hinduization or sankskritization process, he says, "was a civilizing one, detribasation [or detribalization] being its main current bringing about marked changes in the socio religious life of the otherwise tribal people."[27] In other words, sanskritization was a process of detribalization of the previously "tribal" people. The infiltration of the Indic culture into the "otherwise tribal people" by assimilation or conversion into Hinduism civilizes the "tribal" people, which centuries later resulted in their non-tribal identity. Therefore, it is safe to say that Hinduism or its "Indic" culture is a major factor in defining who is a tribal and a non-tribal in Northeast India.

The problem with tribal identity in India, which is an official identity derived from the Constitution of India, is that no single feature can be taken to be normative in defining the "tribes." Nowhere in the Constitution do we find a definition. Article 342 simply says that the President of India can "specify the tribes or tribal communities ... to be Scheduled Tribes" and that the Parliament also has the power to include and exclude groups to and from the list. To justify the enlistment of communities under the "Scheduled Tribes," the government of India did create several criteria. This may have been done surreptitiously, for its existence is not widely known. The list of criteria includes "tribal language, animism, primitivity, hunting and gathering, 'carnivorous in food habits,' 'naked or semi naked,' and fond of drinking and dance'."[28] The list, in my opinion, is simply absurd; and the criteria do not simply match those enlisted. Jaganath Pathy's lamentation is most appropriate. "Not only that over 90 percent of the enlisted groups do not subscribe to these features, but also the criteria [itself] conveys the blatant prejudice of the dominant people."[29] André Béteille's words best expressed the situation in my opinion. He says,

> Ethnographic material from India did not figure prominently in the general discussion regarding the definition of tribe. The problem in India [or the task of the anthropologists] was to identify rather than define tribes, and scientific or theoretical considerations were never allowed to displace administrative or political ones....
>
> Indian anthropologists have been conscious of a certain lack of fit between what their discipline defines as 'tribe' and what they are obliged to describe as 'tribes', but they have sought a way out of the muddle by calling them all 'tribes in transition'.[30]

A close scrutiny of the Constitution reveals that the term is used to designate a whole cluster of diverse non-Indic communities who are mostly non-Aryan and who have remained aloof from the Hindu *varna* or *jati* (caste or colour). Thus, the tribal people may simply be defined as those who are outside the *varna* system of Hindu identification. Furthermore, one also notices that wherever a section on "Scheduled Tribes" appear in the Constitution, a "Scheduled Caste" section appears with similar descriptions and privileges bestowed. If those identified as Scheduled Caste (or Dalit) are people living in close proximity with the Caste people, the tribal people (Scheduled Tribe) are those with no relation with the Caste people for they live far away from the latter. In some cases, tribal people in central India are often described as people living in isolation from mainstream society.

Despite the fact that some of the so-called "tribal" are the most literate communities of India, the Constitution clubbed them together with others under this derogatory name. Why does the Constitution choose this derogatory term? What implications can we draw from this choice? The anomaly of the category of the "Scheduled Tribes", its usage, as well as the identities clustered within its category need to be recognized and acknowledged. The so-called "tribals" of Northeast India and the rest of India have very few features in common. The difference between them is as great a difference as between the "tribals" of the Northeast and the non-tribals of the rest of India. Again the question is why are they being clubbed together? The framers of the Constitution seem to be aware of the difference when they group the Northeast "tribals" separately under the Sixth Schedule and the rest of the "tribals" under the Fifth Schedule of the Constitution.[31] This grouping, however, seems to have been done merely to create separate administrative blocks for different administrative styles fitted to the context.

For the adoption of the nomenclature called "Scheduled Tribes", I find what I call socio-religious explanation to be most convincing. What the framers of the Constitution wished to accomplish, consciously or subconsciously, is to find a place for these diverse communities who "stood more or less outside the Hindu civilization"[32] in relation to the existing caste structure. Thus, by identifying these communities outside of what M. N. Srinivas and R. D. Sanwal called the "socio-ritual hierarchy" (or caste system) of the national mainstream,[33] the "tribals" are indirectly caught up in the prevalent caste structure of the Indian society. In the case of the North easterners, as we have said, assimilation into the Indic culture through Hinduization was the major factor to determine whether a group is called a tribe or a non-tribe.

Ethnonational Feeling and "Tribal" Identity

To a member of the Indian national mainstream, a Khasi, a Naga, a Kuki, or a Mizo are "tribals." The pejorative term "tribal" carries a denotation of primitiveness and inferiority of the people for whom the name is applied. As we have indicated before, in referring to the people as "Scheduled Tribes," the Constitution of India also categorically equates them with the "Scheduled Castes." Consciously or unconsciously, the "tribals" are reduced to the lowest level of the socio-ritual hierarchy of the Indic cultural system. For the simple reason that they are non-Indic and remain outside the traditional Hindu *varna/jati*, they are placed alongside the "outcastes" of the Hindu caste system. Such a detrimental categorization is not acceptable to the proud Northeast "tribes." At the scholarly level, there are a few attempts to understand and to explain the distinctive case of the non-Hindu "tribals" of the Northeast,[34] but in the national majority's understanding, a tribal is a tribal. The attitude of the national mainstream that primitivizes and thereby inferiorizes the "tribals" is in serious conflict with the proud self-understanding of the tribal people in the Northeast. Such a pride, as indicated above, is exhibited in their ethnonational feeling. The people's experience of being despised as "untouchables" and their fear of losing their identity were the major factor that led to ethnopolitical movements of insurgency. In tracing the historical development of insurgency in Nagaland, Asoso Yonuo attributes the people's unpleasant experience of interaction with the "non-tribals" to be one of the main causes of the revolution. The Naga National Council's original demand was "some sort of regional autonomy," he says, and in the course of their interaction with the "non-tribals" they developed the fear of "losing their identity ... in the midst of Hindu rule" leading to a demand for "outright sovereign independent Nagaland state."[35] The people's experience was crucial in the evolution of ethnonational feeling and the spirit of separatism.

> [The] separatist tendency had evolved mainly because of the treatment meted out to them by the converted Hindus and Muslims in Assam and Manipur who regarded them as 'untouchables' or 'dirties,' for their religion and food habits.... The Hindus in the plains of Assam and Manipur despised them for their eating beef and the Muslims pork, for the Nagas ate both.[36]

Resenting their being placed at the most inferior rank through their "tribal" identity, the North easterners have also developed a strong defensive mechanism. The evolution of the ethnonational feeling is largely a defence mechanism. In response to the disdainful treatment they received, the so-called tribal people of the Northeast deprecate and disparage Indic people using pejorative words to describe them. For a Khasi, the word is *dkhar*, for a Tangkhul Naga, *mayang*, for an Ao Naga, *tsümar*, and for a Mizo, *vai*. These are some of the "disparaging terms" the Northeast tribal groups use "to denote their [non-tribal] compatriots."[37]

Toward Developing Mutuality in a Christian Spirit – A Concluding Thought

This chapter is a modest attempt to highlight the complexities of ethnopolitics in Northeast India. Both external and the internal factors are likely to have played significant roles in the creation of the political pandemonium. The external factor, namely, the labelling of the people as "tribal" with all its religio-cultural implications, and the internal factor of ethnonational self-understanding need to be addressed and assessed for any attempt towards long-term solution. A major cause of the ethnopolitical movements of Northeast India is traced to the identity crisis, which is rooted, *inter alia*, in the conflict with the spirit or mind-set that imposed "tribal" identity on the otherwise proud, innovative, and freedom-loving people. An honest recognition of the pain and harm caused by the marginalization and domination through the imposition of a derogative identity is postulated for a harmonious future of the region. In a similar spirit, the North easterners also need to self-critically examine the practice of stereotypical constructions of the image of the "outsiders." Between the national mainstream and the Northeast "tribal" people, a mutual acceptance of the racial-cultural and worldview differences in the spirit of respect and a dialogical discourse in an attempt to enter each other's self-understandings are essential for the future of Indian "nationalism" in Northeast India. For the Christians of Northeast India, the best place to begin such a quest, perhaps, is the church.

In the context of ethnopolitical problems in Northeast India, theologians and religious leaders have often found themselves in a state of quandary. The situation, however, demands appropriate theological responses and directions. Church leaders in some of the states have done marvellous works. Let me end this chapter by suggesting only two themes for future theological explorations by students of Northeast India theology. First, a helpful pathway to the future of the region would be a contextual theological analysis of cultural plurality in the search for mutuality between the so-called in-group and out-group. I strongly suggest that the universality of the Gospel and the catholicity of the Church should be reconsidered and re-evaluated contextually. Secondly, I suggest what anthropologist Victor Turner calls "liminality"[38] (from Latin *limen* or threshold) as a relevant theological theme for the liminal Mongoloid "tribals" of Northeast India. The "betwixt and between" condition of socio-political existence calls for a theological affirmation and embracement. A few works on liminality as a theological theme have come out.[39] In analysing the marginalization of the people, the liminal condition of existence needs to be the starting point. For the "neither this nor that" circumstance of the Northeastern "tribals," liminality as a theological theme, therefore, deserves attention.

Endnotes

[1] R. A. Schermerhorn, *Ethnic Plurality in India* (Tucson: University of Arizona Press, 1978), 86.

[2] See John Hutchinson, "Cultural Nationalism and Moral Regeneration," in *Nationalism*, Oxford Readers, eds. J. Hutchinson and A. D. Smith, Oxford and New York: Oxford University Press, 1994, 122-131.

[3] This is a popular concept in India as Hindutva. For a broader discussion at a global level, see Mark Juergensmeyer, *The New Cold War? Religious Nationalism Confronts the Secular State* (Berkeley: University of California Press, 1993).

[4] See Walker Connor, *Ethnonationalism: The Quest for Understanding* (Princeton, NJ: Princeton University Press, 1994).

[5] Connor, Ibid, xi, 93-94.

[6] Carmen A. Abubakar, "The Moro Ethno-nationalist Movement," in *Ethnicity: Identity, Conflict, Crisis*, eds. D. Kumar and S. Kadirgamar (Hongkong: Arena Press, 1989), 109; quoted in Anjan Ghosh, "Ethnonationalism: A Conceptual Clarification," in *Ethnonationalism: An Indian Experience*, eds. A Ghosh and R. Chakrabarti (Calcutta: Chatterjee Publishers, 1991), 31.

[7] Stanley J. Tambiah, "The Nation-State in Crisis and the Rise of Ethnonationalism," in *The Politics of Difference: Ethnic Premises in a World of Power*, eds. E. N. Wilmsen and P. McAllister (Chicago and London: The University of Chicago Press, 1996), 124.

[8] Ibid., 127-129.

[9] Ibid., 127.

[10] Ibid., 128-29.

[11] G. Aloysius, *Nationalism without a Nation in India* (Delhi, Calcutta, Chennai, Mumbai: Oxford University Press, 1997).

[12] F. S. Downs, *History of Christianity in India*, Volume 5, Part 5, *Northeast India in the Nineteenth and Twentieth Centuries* (Bangalore: The Church History Association of India, 1992), 6.

[13] To acknowledge the fact that the terms "tribe" and "tribal" are foreign words imposed on the people with the accompanying pejorative connotations, these terms are used with quotation marks in this book.

[14] Ananda C, Bhagabati, "Emergent Tribal Identity in North-East India," in *Tribal Development in India: Problems and Prospects*, eds. B. Chaudhuri (Delhi: Inter-India Publications, 1982), 218.

[15] Downs, 6.

[16] In scholarly estimation, this great epic poem reached its final form no later than 200 A.D. See, for instance, Thomas J. Hopkins, *The Hindu Religious Traditions* (Belmont, CA: Wadsworth Publishing Co., 1971), 81.

[17] Bangovinda Parampanthi, "Aryanisation and Assimilation of Assam," in *Nation-Building and Development in North East India*, ed. Udayon Misra (Guwahati: Purbanchal Prakash, 1991), 106.

[18] R. N. Mosahary, "Aryanisation and Hinduisation of the Bodos," *Proceedings of the North ast India History Association*, Tenth Session (Shillong: NEIHA, 1989), 165.

[19] According to Sir Edward Gait, the earliest known settlers in the Brahmaputra valley are the the mongoloid Kacharis, whose language is Tibeto-Burman. See Gait, *A History of Assam*, 2nd ed. (Guwahati: Lawyer's Book Stall, 1926 [reprint 1994]), 2, 236.

[20] Mosahary, 167.

[21] The myth of origin of the Tipra Rajah is fully Hindu in character. See A. Mackenzie, *The North-East Frontier of India* (New Delhi: Mittal Publications, 1884 [reprinted 1995]), 269-70.

[22] Saroj Nalini Parratt, *The Religion of Manipur: Beliefs, Rituals and Historical Development* (Calcutta: Firma KLM Pvt. Ltd., 1980), 103, 113, 141ff.

[23] *Encyclopedia of Religion and Ethics*, ed. James Hastings, s.v. "Manipuris" by T. C. Hodson.

[24] Nibaran Bora, "Insurgency in the North-East," in *Political Development of the North-East*, Volume ii, ed., B. C. Bhuyan (New Delhi: Omsons Publications, 1992), 1.

[25] For a fuller discussion on this, see Lalsangkima Pachuau, *Ethnic Identity and Christianity: A Socio-Historical and Missiological Study of Christianity in Northeast India with Special Reference to Mizoram* (Frankfurt am Main: Peter Lang, 2002; Bangalore: Centre for Contemporary Christianity, 2012), 34-43.

[26] M. Horam, *Naga Insurgency: The Last Thirty Years* (New Delhi: Cosmo Publications, 1988), 21-30.

[27] Ramesh Burgohain, "Cross-Currents of the Hinduisation Process in Medieval Assam," *The Proceedings of the North East India History Association*, Tenth Session (Shillong: NEIHA, 1989), 177.

[28] The list of criteria is quoted from Jaganath Pathy, "The Idea of Tribe in the Indian Scene," *Tribal Transformation in India*, Vol. III, *Ethnopolitics and Identity Crisis*, ed., B. Chaudhuri (New Delhi: Inter-India Publications, 1992), 49.

[29] Ibid.

[30] André Béteille, "The Concept of Tribe with Special Reference to India," *Archives Européennes de Sociologie* 27 (1986): 299.

[31] P. K. Bose divides all of the tribal regions into "two territorial zones," namely, "the north-eastern or frontier zone and the non-frontier zone." See P. K. Bose, "Congress and the Tribal Communities in India," in *Diversity and Dominance in India*, Vol. 2, *Division, Deprivation and the Congress*, eds. R. Roy and R. Sisson (New Delhi: Sage Publications, 1990), 64.

[32] Béteille, 316.

[33] M. N. Srinivas and R. D. Sanwal, "Some Aspects of Political Development in the North-Eastern Hill Areas of India," in *The Tribal Situation in India*, ed. K. S. Singh (Shimla: Indian Institute of Advanced Study, 1972), 121.

[34] For instance, in his book *The Scheduled Tribes*, 3rd ed. (Bombay: Popular Prakashan, 1963), G. S. Ghurye admitted that the "Scheduled Tribes" of the Northeast need to be treated separately. He brought out a separate study on the Northeast *The Burning Caldron of North-East India* (Bombay: Popular Prakashan, 1980).

[35] Asoso Yonuo, *The Rising Nagas: A Historical and Political Study* (Delhi: Vivek Publishing House, 1974), 166.

[36] Ibid., 168.

[37] V. I. K. Sarin, *India's North-East in Flames* (Ghaziabad, UP: Vikash Publishing House, 1982), 254-55.

[38] Victor W. Turner, *The Ritual Process: Structure and Anti-Structure* (Chicago: Aldine Publishing Company, 1969), 94-130.

[39] For instance, see Mark Kline Taylor, "In Praise of Shaky Ground: The Liminal Christ and Cultural Pluralism," *Theology Today* 43 (April, 1986): 36-51.